THE BURNING HEART
OF THE WORLD

THE
BURNING HEART
OF THE WORLD

a novel

Nancy Kricorian

Red Hen Press | *Pasadena, CA*

Book design by Mark E. Cull.

Library of Congress Cataloging-in-Publication Data

Names: Kricorian, Nancy, author.
Title: The burning heart of the world: a novel / Nancy Kricorian.
Description: First edition. | Pasadena, CA: Red Hen Press, 2025.
Identifiers: LCCN 2024037620 (print) | LCCN 2024037621 (ebook) |
ISBN 9781636281933 (paperback) | ISBN 9781636281964 (ebook)
Subjects: LCGFT: Novels.
Classification: LCC PS3561.R52 B87 2025 (print) | LCC PS3561.R52
(ebook)
 | DDC 813/.54—dc23/eng/20240816
LC record available at https://lccn.loc.gov/2024037620
LC ebook record available at https://lccn.loc.gov/2024037621

The National Endowment for the Arts, the Los Angeles County Arts
Commission, the Ahmanson Foundation, the Dwight Stuart Youth
Fund, the Max Factor Family Foundation, the Pasadena Tournament
of Roses Foundation, the Pasadena Arts & Culture Commission and
the City of Pasadena Cultural Affairs Division, the City of Los Angeles
Department of Cultural Affairs, the Audrey & Sydney Irmas Charita-
ble Foundation, the Meta & George Rosenberg Foundation, the Albert
and Elaine Borchard Foundation, the Adams Family Foundation, Am-
azon Literary Partnership, the Sam Francis Foundation, and the Mara
W. Breech Foundation partially support Red Hen Press.

First Edition
Published by Red Hen Press
www.redhen.org

To James

CONTENTS

My heart is like a house in ruins,
the beams in splinters, the pillars shaken.
Wild birds build their nest where my home once was.

—Gomidas

MOUNT LEBANON

The family climbed into the silver Peugeot the father had borrowed from a neighbor for a rare excursion to the mountains. The parents slid into the leather upholstered seats in the front, while the grandmother and three children squeezed into the back. The car wended through Beirut's narrow and crowded streets, then moved north along the coastal highway, turning onto the steep road behind the Armenian Cathedral.

As the car ascended into the mountains, the smallest boy, thumb in his mouth, dozed in his grandmother's lap. The other boy craned his neck out the window as they passed through a village where old stone houses squatted alongside the road. A boy sitting on a milk crate outside a market waved and the girl waved back. Approaching the next village, the father slowed as a flock of goats crossed the road. They rolled past clusters of stone pines and stands of oaks with leaves shimmering in the afternoon light. Finally, they reached Bologna, a small village nestled in a grove of tall conifers, stopping in front of the whitewashed home of some distant cousins.

The couple, who had no children, greeted them at the door. The woman, her gray hair drawn back into a bun, pinched the girl's cheek too hard, smoothed flat the older brother's unruly hair, and when she leaned down to kiss the little one, he skittered behind his mother's skirt.

Dinner was served on a broad balcony overlooking a valley where a row of umbrella pines stood like sentinels and the red tile roofs of another hilltop village could be seen in the distance. Heaping plates were set before the children, and soon their bellies were so full that there was barely room for the sweets that were proffered.

As the hostess poured thick coffee into small porcelain cups, the children were dismissed from the table.

"Take this flashlight. It will be dark soon," the host said, handing the silver torch to the girl, who as the eldest was the appointed leader.

The children, who seldom left the city, dashed out of the house, running beyond the carpet of pine needles to search for grasshoppers in the tall grass. They saw bats winging through the twilight and heard the call of an owl from deep inside the forest. As the last light dropped from the sky, the darkness was filled with the noise of cricket choirs and barking dogs. When the moon appeared above the pines and a strange howling rose in the distance, the younger boy reached for his sister's hand. The children were already walking toward the house when they heard their mother call to them from the balcony.

In the guest bedroom, the parents took their places in the old oak bed, the grandmother settled onto a cot, and the children nestled among quilts and blankets on the floor. The girl lay between her brothers. The bedding smelled of mothballs and the floorboards were hard, but it had been a long day and soon the boys were asleep. She listened to the pulsing chorus of the crickets outside.

The girl opened her eyes. Sunlight was seeping through the slats of the wooden shutters. She heard a dull thudding coming from afar.

"Are you awake?" the older brother whispered.

She nodded. "Where's the little one?"

"He's in the big bed," the boy said. "Everyone's asleep. Let's go."

She slipped her dress over her head, he tugged pants over his pajamas, and they pulled on their jackets. They carried their shoes, putting them on just outside the front door. They made their way through the pine grove near the house, following the road until they arrived at the edge of a clearing with a view of the far mountain range. High above, hundreds of birds flew in great formations. The girl thought that they resembled rows of black letters streaming across the sky.

Suddenly there was a loud blast that echoed through the valley, and then another blast and another. Her brother raced toward the sound.

"Armen," she called. "Where are you going?"

She chased after him, worried that he would get hurt and that her mother would blame her.

Ahead of them, Vera, that was her name, saw a group of men and older boys with rifles raised heavenward, aiming at the passing flocks. With one shot after the next, birds plummeted to the ground, and the boys who were too small to handle the guns scurried to retrieve the bodies. The boys lined up the trophies on the hoods of their fathers' cars. After depositing two birds, one small boy, who had to stand on tiptoe to reach the car, wiped his fingers on his shirtfront, smearing red across the yellow fabric.

As the shooting went on, Vera felt the thud of each bullet in her body. She stared at the bundles of sodden feathers. So many birds, different sizes, varied plumages, only minutes before winging through the skies, and now all of them lifeless. The bullets were relentless, and the birds continued to drop.

Just then a large white bird plummeted from the sky, thumping heavily against the ground not far from the girl's feet. Its long neck was twisted, the narrow red beak bright on the dirt, its black-tipped white wings spread awkwardly as they had fallen, and the white breast feathers were spattered with blood.

They are murderers, the girl thought. All of them are murderers. The killing must stop.

Her brother yelled, "Vera, shut up! Do you hear me? Shut up."

Dazed, she looked at her brother, standing amidst the gathered men and boys, all of them now staring at her. She hadn't even realized that she was shouting. But, at least for a moment, the shooting had ended.

NEW YORK CITY

The sky was an infinite blue and sun glinted off storefront windows as Vera and George walked south on Broadway. When they turned toward the park, a man bobbed up on the sidewalk ahead of them.

"Did you see the big holes in the buildings?" he asked. "I saw it on the drive up here."

Vera scanned his face. He seemed rational. She looked down at the name embroidered on his blue work shirt. Hector.

George said, "What?"

Hector said, "The Twin Towers. One plane could be an accident, but two?"

He veered right, disappearing into the service entrance of an apartment building.

George said, "That was a bit nutty."

Ahead of them on Central Park West, a string of police trucks barreled south with blue wooden barricades rattling in the back. A line of white police cruisers followed, their lights spinning and sirens shrieking.

Behind the lobby desk of their psychotherapist's building, the doorman in his navy suit with gold buttons was leaning over a transistor radio tuned to the news. Recognizing them, he waved them past.

The elevator operator silently pushed the brass control handle to the left, keeping his back to Vera and George.

On the seventeenth floor, George rang the bell, and they entered the therapist's apartment through its unlocked front door. The live-in housekeeper, a tall woman in a crimson housecoat, said, "She's waiting for you."

Elderly Dr. Letty Green was enthroned in her Eames chair.

"Good morning," Letty said, smiling.

George asked, "Did you hear anything about the Twin Towers?"

"Delia mentioned something was going on down there," Letty said.

George gestured at the television in the corner of the room. "Maybe we could see what's happening."

Letty said, "It's broken. Take a seat so we can begin."

Out of the south-facing picture window behind the therapist's chair, Vera saw some men standing on a nearby rooftop. One of them was pointing at what looked like two pillars of gray smoke rising at the far end of the island.

Letty said, "Let's start where we left off last time. We were discussing Vera's need for control and order, and the effect that has on the family."

Just then the housekeeper knocked on the door. "Sorry to interrupt. I just heard on the news that the towers collapsed. They shut down the subways."

There was a brief silence in the room.

Vera glanced at her watch. The twins had only a short phase in that morning—it was their first week at school. She said, "Oh dear. Maybe Annette didn't make it in time to pick up the kids."

As George and Vera hit the sidewalk, fighter jets scrambled overhead. George hailed a taxi. He slid across the seat and Vera climbed in after him. The driver was listening to a frantic radio report with the volume on high.

"I was down there," the driver said. "They were jumping. They hit the pavement like water balloons."

Vera pressed her fingers to her eyelids and saw red. Then a stream of objects floated past: an eyeless baby doll, a nest of tangled electrical wires, and a dead cat.

She felt George's hand on her shoulder. "Vera?"

"I'm okay," she said.

When they reached the school, George told her, "While you get the kids, I'll head to the bank for cash."

She nodded. "I'll stop for groceries on the way home. Can you go to the hardware store?"

"What do you need?" George asked.

"Another flashlight, some batteries, candles, and matches."

"Expecting a hurricane?" George asked.

"Humor me," she said.

Vera peered into Sophie's classroom. Many of the kids had already been collected, and those who remained sat at the low round tables drawing. The teacher came to the door and said, "Sophie left with Annette." Vera crossed the hall, poking her head into Simon's classroom. The teacher nodded to confirm that he too had been picked up.

She hurried to the grocery store, where shoppers steered their carts around each other as though it were a racetrack with no agreed upon finish line. She grabbed cans of chickpeas and diced tomatoes from the shelves. She rolled down the narrow aisles snatching more items at random: a carton of long-life milk, a jar of peanut butter, yogurt, bananas, apples, a head of cabbage, two chickens, chocolate bars, and an assortment of batteries. You could never have too many batteries. The radio, she thought. Do we have a transistor radio?

Vera helped the twins build a fort in the dining room, draping a sheet over the table and pinning its corners to four chairs. The kids crawled in and arranged pillows and toys under the table.

Vera carried the cordless phone to the kitchen.

"Thank God you are alive!" her mother said in a torrent of Armenian. "I couldn't get through to you. I finally reached Raffi. He said he's good, but I don't believe him. He lives too close to there. Thank God that Armen and his family are in New Jersey near us. Are you safe? How are the twins?"

"We are safe," she answered in Armenian.

"What about George?"

"He never went to the office. We dropped the kids at school, and he was uptown with me."

Sophie ran into the kitchen. "Mama, Simon spilled his juice box on my pillow."

Simon dashed in behind her. "It was her fault. She made me spill it."

Sophie said, "I did not. You're a liar."

"I'll call you later," Vera told her mother.

The afternoon dragged itself toward dinnertime. Vera and George took turns sneaking into their bedroom to watch the small portable TV perched atop the dresser. With the bedroom door locked, Vera stared at the footage of the second plane as it slammed into the South Tower. The ball of orange flames turned into churning clouds of smoke. And then they showed it again from a different angle. And another.

Once the twins were asleep, George turned on the news in the living room, but Vera could not stand to see it one more time, so she went to bed.

In the middle of the night, she bolted awake, her blood pulsing wildly. For a few seconds she didn't know where she was. She saw in the dark above her a car engulfed in flames and heard an explosion that shattered the windowpanes. The war was sharp on her like a knife. She saw an old man lying on the ground. He was wearing a long blue and white striped tunic with a black vest over it and baggy black pants. There was a ragged red hole just above his eyebrow, and dark blood pooled under his head. His eyes were open as though he were staring at the heavens. Scattered around him on the dusty pavement were cured black olives fallen from a sack he had been carrying. His lips moved, and she heard him whisper, "How could you have forgotten me?"

When the morning paper thumped onto the mat, Vera opened the door to the flaming towers. Below the fold, firefighters stood shoulder to shoulder in the rubble. Red rivulets ran down a dust-coated face. She read in tiny print that the day would be sunny with a few afternoon clouds and a high of 77 degrees.

She rolled up the paper, wedging it under her arm. She was tempted to stuff it in the trash, but George would want to see it, so she slid it into the bottom drawer of the credenza in the front hall.

Schools were closed and so was George's office, which was located eight blocks north of the Trade Center. He was holed up in the maid's room that served as Vera's studio. She wouldn't be able to work anyway. Who would watch the kids? How could she concentrate?

She heard George's muffled voice through the closed door.

After breakfast the kids lolled on the couch in their pajamas, watching cartoons on the big television. In the late morning her mother called, her volume increasing as they talked. Her mother was sure there would be more attacks. She was sure that Vera, George, and the twins were about to be murdered if they weren't already dead.

Her mother shouted, "Come out here now! Go to your brother's house. He said you can stay in the apartment over the garage for as long as you want."

Vera said, "The bridges and tunnels are closed."

Her mother said, "It's a madhouse. What comes next? Car

bombs? Kidnapping? We left Beirut to get away from this kind of craziness, and here it is falling on our heads again."

Vera held the receiver away from her ear. Her mother sounded like a wheezing, whistling starling. Vera wondered how far the pigeons near the disaster site had flown. All she remembered about birds during the war in Lebanon was Shakar, her grandmother's canary, and how listless he was when they were trapped inside the underground bomb shelter for a week.

After lunch, the kids shimmied out of their pajamas. Simon pulled on shorts and a T-shirt. Sophie flounced out in a flowered dress over polka-dotted pants. Vera carried a canvas tote filled with toys and snacks as they headed to the playground. The atmosphere along the park drive was surreally calm. There were very few cars on the road.

Kids pumped their legs on the swings, or they clambered up and flung themselves down the slide. Sophie and Simon planted themselves with plastic buckets and shovels in the sandbox. Meanwhile, mothers clustered in small groups talking in the hushed tones reserved for divorce or terminal illness. Their stories eddied around Vera.

"He was in the South Tower. He called his wife just as they were evacuating, and no one has heard from him since."

"She was supposed to be on the United plane out of Logan. At the last minute she changed her flight for one later in the day."

"His office is in 7 World Trade. He looked like a zombie when he finally got home. I told him to go to bed early because he was scaring the kids."

Vera moved to a bench at the edge of the playground. Scanning for the twins, she spotted Sophie sitting on the climbing structure's bridge with another little girl, the two of them engrossed in conversation. Simon and a band of small boys were excavating a pit in the sandbox.

A flock of sparrows flitted in the low bushes and foraged in the grass. The male house sparrows had little black goatees. She closed her eyes, pressing her back against the slats of the wooden bench. The military helicopters above sounded like hornets. The wind must have shifted because she smelled smoke. An acrid taste in her mouth transported her to Beirut. A pillar of fire singed the air and automatic weapons stuttered in the distance. *Karantina, oh Karantina.*

She felt a small hand on her knee. She opened her eyes onto the sight of her daughter's worried face framed by glossy dark hair.

"Are you sleeping?" Sophie asked.

"I was resting," Vera said.

Sophie said, "Ariel told me the bad guys came from New Jersey. What if when you aren't looking, someone tries to kidnap me?'

She pulled Sophie toward her, resting her face against her child's warm cheek. Her daughter smelled like baby shampoo and dirt. It was Vera's task to protect this small body, but for a moment she was using her child as a shield.

In the steeply raked auditorium, Vera found a seat on the aisle toward the back. The kids were in their classrooms, and the parents had been invited to discuss "the week's events" with the school psychologist.

Dr. Dora Diamond told them, "This is a scary time, and how you talk with your children is crucial to their well-being. Answer only the specific question being asked as briefly as possible. The main thing is to reassure them that you will keep them safe."

When the floor was opened for questions a father asked, "How are we supposed to keep them safe when there are lunatics flying planes into buildings?"

Dr. Diamond said, "Some things are too frightening for your kids to process. Keep them away from violent images on TV and in the newspaper."

"Why do they hate us?" another woman asked. She burst into tears.

Vera scanned the faces around her. Their features were strange and distorted, and the voices echoed as though they were coming from the bottom of a deep well. Was it her imagination, or were some of the other parents casting wary glances at her?

She stopped listening and closed her eyes. Memories darted through her mind like minnows in a brook. She and her younger brother Raffi sat on the curb while their grandmother swept the sidewalk in front of their house. She heard the straw broom rasp against the pavement, and the voices of her brother Armen and his friends playing ball in the street. Suddenly she was no longer her present self, the one sitting in a hall full of anxious, angry strangers, but she was that other Vera, the one she had left behind in Beirut.

Vera and her college friend Emily, whose painting studio was in the basement of her Brooklyn brownstone, had regular Friday phone dates. That morning Emily told Vera that when she had heard about the first plane over the radio, she had climbed to the roof in time to see the other plane slam into the second tower.

Emily said, "It was like a special effects scene in a disaster movie. I decided right then to get my kids. On the drive to the school, I had a clear view of the towers. After they collapsed, scraps of paper and ash fell on the car. Then a finger landed on the windshield."

Vera said, "A finger?"

Emily said, "Yeah. A finger. On the way home the wind was blowing south. There was so much smoke and dust it was like driving through fog."

"Jeannie told me the dust is filled with toxins. You should have your house tested, especially the roof."

"Jesus, think about the computers, thousands of them, and all that jet fuel. I can't talk about this. I haven't been able to paint. I can't focus on anything for more than ten minutes."

Later, when the phone rang, it was Vera's cousin Arda, who lived in New Jersey and worked in the financial district.

Arda said in Armenian, "I just heard the worst story."

Vera braced herself.

Arda continued, "My friend's cousin was in the tower when the first plane hit. They all ran for the exits. The police ordered them back to their desks so they wouldn't block the stairwells for the firefighters."

While she listened, Vera slid the elements of the collage she was working on around the paper: a ballet dancer in an organza skirt, a bouquet of roses, a flight of swallows, and pieces of a striped grosgrain ribbon. She imagined setting a match to the whole thing.

Arda went on, "They all went back to their desks, except my friend's cousin. She sneaked out. She was a few blocks away when the towers fell. Everyone else is gone."

That night after the kids were in bed, Vera and George sat at the dining room table paying bills. She wrote the checks, and he slid them into envelopes, then stamped and sealed them. While they were working, she recounted both stories she had heard that day. She was fixated on the image of the finger on the windshield, and she was haunted by the idea that people who did as they were told ended up dead.

She said, "I'm afraid I would have gone back to my desk."

"You would have run," George said. "I guarantee you would have run."

Vera wished she could be so sure.

She thought about her mother's father, who had decided not to return to his hometown after the First World War. The Armenians who had survived the Deportations and returned to Hadjin had held off the Turks for several months in 1920. "In the end, they butchered them like sheep," her grandfather had said.

How could you know when it was time to flee? How would you have the courage to disobey the orders? How would you decide to turn right on the road rather than left? Only later would it be clear that one path had meant survival and the other had led to a mass grave in the desert.

Vera snapped at Simon when he knocked over his glass of milk. She was exhausted. The night before she had been awakened after midnight by her son's small face hovering over her. "I had an accident," he whispered. She led him back to his bed and changed the sheets.

While she was at the sink after dinner, her yellow rubber gloves covered with suds, she turned down Sophie's request for help buttoning a doll's dress.

"When I finish the dishes . . ." Vera started to say.

Sophie interrupted, "All you do is dishes, dishes, dishes. You are no fun at all. You never want to play with us anymore."

In the weeks since the attacks, Vera's gut churned at the scuttering sound of police helicopters, or sirens howling on the avenues. She was gripped by stories about The Pile and The Pit, where they continued unearthing human remains while noxious smoke and dust filtered through the city. When they said they were going to bomb Afghanistan back to the Stone Age, she imagined Afghan women and children huddling in caves as hell rained down on them. She also feared there would be retaliation.

"We live in the capital city of the empire, the number one target," George said. "Beirut on the Hudson."

She flinched at the mention of Beirut. The war was alive in her again. Lately she almost dreaded going to sleep, not knowing what violent scenes might play out in the theater of her dreams.

She was walking up Broadway. The sky was dim and thick

with black smoke. The streets were empty except for a lone red fire truck, its siren shrilling as it headed south. The storefronts were shuttered. She entered the door of a small ice cream shop, the only store that was open. There was a tall young clerk, bespectacled and pale, behind the counter. He had a radio pressed to one ear.

She asked him, "What happened?"

He said, "They're shelling Midtown, and the land invasion has begun."

She tore out of the shop, needing to get home to her children, but there were no buses, no taxis, no cars. She started running, and then she was no longer in Manhattan. She was on the bridge between Bourj Hammoud and Nor Hadjin. There were crumpled and bloodied bodies strewn on the pavement ahead of her. She dodged around them, struggling to advance, but no matter how hard she tried she was unable to make headway. Nor Hadjin was within sight but impossible to reach. Suddenly fingers started dropping from the sky, slapping the pavement around her. She shielded her face with her arm, afraid that one of them would hit her.

Vera woke, her heart heaving, her breath quick and shallow.

George switched on the bedside lamp. "Another bad dream?"

She said, "It wasn't that bad."

"That's the third time this week," he said.

"Everyone's having nightmares. Seems like a reasonable response."

"Right," he said, "but it seems like it's a little worse for you. Maybe you want to talk to Letty on your own?"

"I'm okay, really, I am fine," she said.

"You know that isn't convincing, right? You seem totally phased out lately."

"Well, you were complaining about my being bossy and controlling, and now you're complaining that I'm phased out."

"I'm not complaining," he said. "I'm worried."

Vera was supposed to drive with the twins to New Jersey for Sunday dinner with her family. Maybe someone had planted a bomb on the bridge, which would blow up as they were passing over the middle of the river. The car would tumble into the water and sink as she struggled to free her kids. They would all drown, and George would be a childless widower. Better he should go with them so he could rescue them, or they would all die together.

"Are you sure you don't want to come?" she asked.

George said, "I need to work today. The spreadsheet is a mess, and I promised I'd get it to Peter by tomorrow."

She said, "I'm scared."

"Why don't you call Raffi," he told her. "I'm sure he would go with you."

Her brother lived downtown with his boyfriend, whose existence was still unacknowledged by their parents. When Vera phoned, she expected that Raffi would tell her he didn't want to waste his Sunday in New Jersey, but instead he agreed.

"That was too easy," she said. "Why?"

"Because you're scared to drive over the bridge alone," Raffi said.

"Did George tell you?" she asked.

Raffi laughed. "I know you, Vera."

A few hours later, she was in the station wagon with Raffi and the kids crossing the Hudson. Sophie and Simon adored their Amo Raffi, who dispensed chewing gum and juggled oranges.

She was glad to hear them speaking Armenian with him. She felt that her mother held her personally responsible for the demise of the Armenian language. Why didn't Vera send her children to Armenian day school the way her brother Armen did? Why didn't she enroll them in Saturday school at the church so they could at least learn the alphabet? She let her mother's harangues wash over her, leaving behind a sticky film of guilt.

Their house was a Cape Cod cottage on a cul-de-sac ten minutes from the bridge. There were two bedrooms plus a narrow sun porch where Vera had slept. There were Oriental carpets, framed family photographs on the mantel and living room walls, and potted plants that her mother transferred outside in summer. Her father had built the furniture in the living room and dining room, carving designs on the walnut legs of the tables and chairs. Her mother had covered the cushions with gold jacquard fabric and had sewn matching curtains.

In the living room, Vera found Armen reading the newspaper. Raffi settled into an armchair next to Armen, and Vera guided the twins ahead of her, following the scent of butter, lamb, and onions to the kitchen. Her mother, wearing a red checked apron and hot mitts, pulled a casserole from the oven. She placed it on the stovetop and bent down to kiss the twins.

"Look how big you are," her mother said in Armenian. "Go find your cousins in the yard."

As the door swung shut behind the kids, she said to Vera, "Is that Raffi I hear? How did you convince him?"

"He came for the food. And I promised you wouldn't ask when he's getting married."

Her mother swatted the air with a hot mitt. "He doesn't need to marry. I have five grandchildren. That's enough. Where is your Greek groom?"

"He had to work."

"On a Sunday? It was lucky he wasn't in his office that day to see those jumpers. Things like that stay with you forever. Remember when the Kataeb tied that Hagopian boy from Khalil Badawi to the back of a jeep?"

"I didn't see that," Vera said, "but you have told me that story so many times it feels like I did."

"Maybe you were at school that day. Then there was the time they killed that boy just outside the club. What was his name? Maybe Koko Marashlian? My memory is terrible these days. They paraded around with his hand on a stick."

"Please don't talk like this in front of my kids. Nothing about the war, or the attacks," she said.

"You better tell your father and Armen. You know how they talk," her mother said.

"Where's Baba?" Vera asked.

"Out in the garage, finishing your boxes."

As she went to find her father, Vera remembered their first days in this house. The transition from Beirut to America had been hard on her. While Raffi went to a nearby Armenian grade school, Vera and Armen were tossed into the town's public schools. She had imitated the popular girls down to the kind of hair ties they used, but she had a foreign accent, and the almost-right clothes always fit her the wrong way.

At one point, Vera had yelled at her mother, "You made us leave everything. You made us come here. You raised us to be short adults. Now I want to be an American teenager."

"What is an American teenager?" her mother shouted at her. "A hooligan? A whore? Do you think you are the only one who has problems? This country is killing your father little by little, but does he complain? We brought you here so you wouldn't be kidnapped and raped by those gangster militias. You should thank me. Go tell your father it's time for dinner."

In the garage, her father was running the lathe. When he saw her, he switched off the machine.

"They're ready," he said, pointing at a stack of wooden boxes on the workbench.

She selected a box from the top of the pile, inspecting the grain of the maple. They were beautifully made, with hidden dovetails and an inner ridge for the glass front she would insert once the interiors of the shadow boxes were complete.

"They're perfect," she said. "Can you make me ten more?"

"I'll have them ready in two weeks." His voice was weary, and there were dark crescents under his eyes.

"You look tired," she said.

He said, "Your mother is keeping me up. She's having nightmares."

"I had no idea. She always acts so tough."

He said, "This is no country for humans. People work all the time. When they aren't working, they lock themselves in their houses surrounded by white fences. It's a land of the lonely."

"You could go back," she said. "The war has been over for ten years."

He shrugged. "Do you think your mother would leave her grandchildren?"

"It's time to eat, Baba," she said.

"You go," he told her. "I'll be five minutes."

As she exited the garage, she heard his voice behind her, "I came here like a wounded bird from a burning country."

In the dining room Vera's mother prepared plates for the children and told them, "Don't wait for me. Eat before it gets cold. Eat. Eat."

Sophie was seated next to her baby cousin Lucy in the high-chair, and Simon sat between his two older cousins. All of them were gabbing away in Armenian.

Their grandmother asked the big boys how they were doing at school.

Their mother answered for them. "They are both at the top of their class."

"What about sports?" their grandfather asked.

David, the younger one, said, "We play in the travel soccer league."

Mark said, "Some boys on the other team said I was a terrorist. They told me to go back to where I came from."

Simon said, "That doesn't make sense. You can't be a terrorist. You don't know how to fly a plane."

The entrance to the bridge was snarled with traffic as they headed back to the city.

"Your kids are drugged on food," Raffi said.

Vera glanced in the rearview mirror and saw that the twins were asleep, their heads tilted and Simon's mouth agape.

"That wasn't so bad," Raffi said. "Armen made only one snide crack."

"I missed it," she said. "What did he say?"

"Nothing new so I'm not going to repeat it."

"He's just jealous."

"Of my wonderful gay downtown life in the exclusion zone," Raffi said.

"How are you doing?" she asked him.

"You know, bad dreams like everyone, but basically managing. How is your couples therapy going?"

"Hard to tell. We were making some progress, I think, but then . . ."

"The Twin Towers," Raffi finished her sentence.

As people hurried past her down the steps, Vera gripped the handrail at the subway entrance. It was her first time going underground since the attack. Trains flowed beneath the city the way blood coursed through the body's net of vessels.

Some people made pilgrimage to the smoking crater at Ground Zero, but not her. She stayed within a five-block radius of their apartment. Recently, George had grown annoyed with her.

"You can't keep pretending the rest of the city doesn't exist," he said.

The silver train shuddered into the station, and a door parted in front of her. She looked at the other passengers. A man in a suit read the paper. A woman in a blue cloth coat clipped her fingernails. An elderly woman ate peanuts out of a small paper bag, dropping their shells and skins into her lap.

She exited the car and navigated through the subterranean hall connecting the web of train lines at Times Square. She skirted a pair of police officers patrolling with a German shepherd. As she proceeded to the next platform, she passed soldiers wearing bulletproof vests over their camouflage uniforms. They carried semiautomatic weapons. Would they check identity cards? Would they drag some hapless soul out of sight to be beaten or worse? She put her hand against a metal pillar to steady herself. The train pulled into the station, and she boarded.

At the restaurant, Mimi, the buyer from the high-end boutique department store that sold Vera's boxes, was already seated. They picked at their salads and exchanged the requisite stories about that fateful morning. After the dishes were cleared, Mimi asked to see what Vera had in her portfolio. Vera pulled out one collage at a time, and Mimi scrutinized each of them, twelve in all, putting four to one side.

"These four will work," Mimi said. "The colors are terrific, and I love the flowers and the birds. You can do variations on these themes. But the other ones." Mimi shuddered. "What's going on, Vera? I know we're all a bit traumatized, but why are there black feathers all over the place? This stuff is way too creepy for us to sell."

Vera glanced at the collage on the top of the reject pile. She realized how disturbing the images were: a pile of dead crows surrounded by loose feathers, and a bonfire filled with flaming snakes.

Mimi continued, "If you want to do dark stuff like that, you should work in large format and find a gallery. There's more room for scary in fine art."

At the Halloween party in their building's lobby, Vera surveyed small wizards, princesses, firefighters, and pirates. Her favorite was a kid dressed as a roll of Lifesavers candy. Sophie was a fairy with a beribboned wand and iridescent wings. Simon, who didn't want to wear a costume, had been wrangled into a red satin cape and had allowed Vera to pin an S to his shirtfront only because he wanted the candy.

The mother who had organized the event announced, "The first group can take the elevator to the top and start making their way down."

Vera, George, and the twins were in a group with four other kids and their parents. A tiny ghost rapped on the door of the first apartment, and they all shouted, "Trick or treat." When they had knocked on all the doors and collected the sweets on that floor, they trooped down the stairs to the one below.

Outside their apartment door, Vera had placed a bowl of chocolate bars on a table. At the other end of the hall their neighbors' door was decorated with cobwebs and an enormous black spider with long furry legs. A sign said, "Knock and enter."

The door opened onto a dark entrance hall where jack-o'-lanterns cast flickering light on the ceiling. Two hunchbacks in trench coats approached, each carrying a brown paper bag, one labeled "Chocolate Eyeballs" and the other "Bloody Fish." The hunchback on the left wore a rubber Frankenstein mask. The other had a hatchet buried in his head and streaks of blood running down his face.

When she opened her eyes, Vera realized that she was lying on the couch in their neighbors' living room. Simon sat in George's lap, and Sophie stood next to Vera stroking her hair. The teenagers had pulled off their masks.

The boys poured candy into Sophie and Simon's buckets.

Their mother said, "I told them that was going to be too much for the little kids."

"We're sorry," the older one said.

His brother added, "We didn't mean to scare you."

Simon said, "You didn't scare us. You scared our mom."

As soon as George left for a two-night work trip to Boston, Vera was afraid she would never see him again. Anything could happen—a train derailment, or a taxicab crash, or even a mass shooting. She suddenly felt as though her life was a garment held together with safety pins.

"We're going to have a sleepover with Babig and Medz Mairig," she told the twins as she helped them into their jackets. "Annette will pick you up from school and bring you to the garage."

"What about my playdate with Amanda?" Sophie asked.

"I'll call her mother and change it to next week," she answered.

When they headed north on the highway, the sky was bright, and gusts churned up white caps on the glittering river. The bridge's cables vibrated, and the bridge itself seemed to sway in the wind.

When they arrived at the back door, Vera's mother asked, "What are you doing here? I didn't know you were coming."

Vera said, "I forgot to call you."

Her mother looked at her strangely. She told the twins, "Come in, come in, my little chicks, before the wind blows you away."

"Is Baba in his workshop?" Simon asked.

"He is," his grandmother said.

They barreled out of the kitchen to find their grandfather.

Her mother said, "Vera, you are skinny as a stick."

Vera sat down at the kitchen table, smoothing her skirt.

"You want some coffee?" her mother asked.

"Tea, please," she said.

While the kettle heated on the stove, Vera leaned back, resting her head against the wall.

"You need to pull yourself together, Vera," her mother said, setting a mug on the table.

"I'm just a little tired."

"The important thing is to stay busy. Keep moving," her mother said. "I'm going to take this tray to the kids."

"Do you need help?" she asked.

"Go get lamb stew from the freezer."

Vera flipped the light switch and descended to the cellar. On the shelves against one wall, there were rows of canned goods. Beans and legumes lined the top shelf, the second shelf had vegetables, and below were tins of sardines and tuna. Canned fruits were arranged on the bottom shelf. The freezer was crammed with chicken, meat, bread, and buckets of soups and stews, plus bags of *manti* and boxes of *lahmajouns* from the local Armenian bakery.

When she set the container of stew on the kitchen counter, Vera commented, "That's a lot of food you have down there."

Her mother said, "I'm ready for anything. You're always welcome here. I have enough for the whole family."

At supper Babig told the kids about the time he had sneaked into the Armenian Brethren churchyard to steal figs. He couldn't take them home, so he sat under the tree and gorged himself. That night as he lay groaning in his bed, he couldn't explain why he was so sick without revealing his crime.

The twins thought this was hilarious.

"Now you teach them to be thieves?" their grandmother said.

He said, "They understand. I stole the figs, and God punished me."

At bedtime Vera sat on a padded stool between the beds in her brothers' old room. She read the kids a fairy tale about a talking fish and sang them an Armenian lullaby. When their lashes finally stilled against their cheeks, she went to the living room to find her parents dozing in the television's flickering blue light. On the old rotary phone in the kitchen, she dialed her in-laws' house outside Boston.

"I tried the apartment, and you didn't answer your mobile," George said.

"I forgot the charger."

"I was worried, Vera. I didn't know where you and the kids were. I was going to call the super to have him check the apartment. You never do things like this."

"I panicked. I didn't want to be there alone with the kids. So I drove to my parents' house."

"How are the twins?" he asked.

"They're fine. They're sleeping. We had a nice dinner."

"You should have let me know where you were," he said.

"I'm sorry. I wasn't thinking."

"I'm cutting the trip short," George said. "I'll be home tomorrow."

"You don't need to do that," Vera said.

"Yes, I do," he told her.

On the sun porch Vera pulled an old flannel nightgown from the chest of drawers. She slid into the narrow bed and drew the chenille spread to her chin. When she closed her eyes, it was as though her mind were cleaved in two. One part of her watched as the other part picked her way down a long, dark stairwell. Her foot slipped on a slick tread, throwing off her balance. She tumbled headlong down the flight of stairs. Suddenly, she was in the underground bomb shelter, lying curled on her side, pressing a pillow over her head as missiles whistled and thudded above. The sound was unbearable. The earth shuddered as a missile struck nearby. She was certain a direct hit would come next. The cement ceiling and pillars would buckle and crumble, and she would be crushed beneath the rubble. Perhaps she was already dead. She felt her lungs expand and contract like a bellows. She must be alive, or at least she was still breathing.

Vera heard the click of the door latch and opened her eyes. Her mother's figure was framed in the doorway with the hall light spilling in around her.

"You're awake," her mother said.

"Yes," she answered.

"Don't let yourself fall apart, Vera," her mother said.

"I don't have your spine of steel."

"But your bones are strong enough." With that, her mother stepped back and closed the door. Vera heard her leather slippers retreat down the hall.

As Vera lay in the dark, headlights from a passing car striped the window shades and disappeared. Then the night was still, and her breath continued slowly in and out of her body, rolling like waves rhythmically approaching and retreating from the beach.

She dreamed she was not far from the shore in Beirut. It was nighttime, and she walked until the Bourj Hammoud garbage mountain loomed ahead. There were fires burning on the mountain's slopes, and smoke smudged the air. Her grandmother was seated in an armchair near the bottom of the mountain. There was a standing lamp beside the chair and in its circle of light her grandmother's head was bent over some handwork.

"Medz Mama," Vera called, "what are you doing here? This isn't heaven."

Her grandmother held up a lace shawl. She said, "I made this for you, *anoushig*. I have loved you all so much."

That evening George had stayed late at the office, and after supper Vera persuaded the kids to join her in her studio. The twins wore parts of their Halloween costumes over their pajamas. Sophie had on her wings, and Simon's cape hung down his back. She set them up on the daybed with coloring books, turning then to her collage table.

She worked on the piece she was calling *Heaven and Hell Are in This World*. She opened one shallow drawer after another, rummaging through her collections for the right elements.

"Are you listening, Mama?" said Sophie. "I'm bored."

"Hmm," she said distractedly. "You want to watch a video?"

The twins were not allowed to watch TV on school nights. She saw Sophie and Simon exchange grins.

Simon jumped up. "Let's go!"

Vera fixed her eyes on the collage. One side was an Edenic garden filled with orchids and parrots, and the other was a war zone where toy soldiers swarmed over a jeep. Something was missing, but she wasn't quite sure what.

She leaned down to pull open the bottom drawer where her grandmother's lace doilies were stored. She lifted a stack of them, spreading them over the tabletop.

Each piece was unique—circles, ovals, stars, flowers, and complicated latticework. The shades ranged from bone white to sand brown. The smallest was the size of a silver dollar and the largest was a long runner for a sideboard. Her grandmother had learned to knot needle lace as a child in the orphanage. Medz Mama said that even though it appeared delicate, the lace was so sturdy that if some of the loops were torn or broken, the rest of the knots would keep the piece from unravelling.

Vera heard Simon yell, "Daddy!"

She heard George ask, "Where's your mother? Where's Sophie?"

Vera went to find them.

"Sophie's in our room," Simon said.

In the bedroom cold air was blowing through the open window that gave onto the fire escape. Sophie was outside leaning precariously over the railing, her wings snapping in the wind.

"I'm flying," the little girl said.

Vera's heart thrashed like a fish on a hook.

"Sosi, come in here this instant," she said. "Sosi! Now!"

George rushed toward Sophie and lifted her in, setting her feet on the carpet.

"Why did you call her Sosi? That's not her name," Simon said.

George rubbed Sophie's hands between his. "You're freezing."

Sophie said, "Look, Daddy. Mama's crying."

George took Vera's shaking hands, drawing her toward him. Her shoulders were heaving, and her breathing was coming in ragged gulps.

"Oh, Vera," George said. He pulled her closer, and she dropped her head onto his shoulder.

Then she glanced down at her children's anxious upturned faces. Guilt flooded through her. She had forgotten them.

"Sorry, my little ones," she said. "Mama's so sorry."

"Okay, kiddos, your mom is tired. Go choose your books and I'll meet you on the couch," George said.

The twins held hands as they left the room, and George turned again to Vera.

"Will you do me a favor?" he asked.

"What?"

"Call Letty."

"Tomorrow," she said. "I promise."

"It's going to be okay," he told her.

Vera left her studio door ajar and gazed out the window at the red, blue, and white lights atop the Empire State Building. The wind was strong, buffeting the panes. From the other room she heard the murmur of George's voice as he read to their children. She picked up the battered alarm clock from the wooden sill, holding its ticking heart to her own. She felt her grandmother standing beside her. She heard her voice saying, *"Gar ou chigar, gar ou chigar."* There was, and there was not.

BEIRUT

Vera and her mother climbed the long flight of steps past the beer factory toward Geitawi hilltop where Cousin Anahid lived.

As they mounted, her mother said, "You met her once when you were small. Her grandmother and my grandmother were first cousins. Her daughter is two years older than you, and the son one year younger."

Her mother paused on the stairs to catch her breath. "You need to be a mountain goat for this hill. But I'm not the one who will have to do this every day. What was I saying? Oh, yes. Anahid agreed to take you if anything happens."

"What does that mean?" Vera asked.

Her mother started up the stairs again. "It means that if for any reason they shut the school in the middle of the day and it isn't safe for you to come home, you go to their apartment, which is right across the street. And you stay there until we come get you, or until it's quiet."

"Overnight?" Vera asked.

"Overnight," her mother said.

"What if the fighting goes on for a month?"

"Why do you always dream up the worst possible thing?"

Vera couldn't stop herself from saying what she was thinking, even though she knew it would further irritate her mother.

"What if a rocket crashes into their apartment and I'm killed? How will you know what happened to me? What if a rocket lands on our house when I'm gone and I'm the only one from our family who survives? I would prefer to die with you."

Her mother pinned Vera with a glare. "Would you prefer to stay home and ruin your eyesight knotting lace doilies with your grandmother?"

Vera said, "I want to go to school."

"Fine. I didn't imagine you as a sixth-grade dropout."

"What about Taline and Seta?"

Her best friends would be starting in the seventh grade at the Central High School with Vera. They had known each other since they were babies, and their friendship was like a three-legged stool. If things were bad and Vera went to stay with her mother's cousin, what would they do?

Her mother said, "You can't expect Anahid to take in the whole neighborhood. Their mothers will make other plans."

Her mother pressed the buzzer, and the door latch clicked open. When they entered the lobby, the lights suddenly went out. As they made their way up the darkened stairwell to the fourth floor, they heard the building's backup generator grind into action, the elevator moved in its shaft, and the hall lights flickered on. When they reached the fourth-floor landing, Cousin Anahid was waiting inside the open door of her apartment.

She said, "Vera, I haven't seen you since you were a baby. Look at what a lovely young lady you have become!"

She was the same age and height as Vera's mother, but she wore makeup and she had plucked off all her eyebrows. In their place she had drawn thick brown crescents, which made her look permanently surprised. Her dress was cut above the knee, and her hair was frosted blond. Her nails were painted a glossy red that matched her lipstick, and she wore a gold necklace, a large diamond ring, and two thick gold bangles.

"Call me Anahid Tantig, honey, and this is Nora. Say hello to your cousin," she instructed her daughter, pushing her forward.

Nora was a miniature version of her mother, with long curling eyelashes and large dark eyes. She hadn't dyed her hair or plucked her eyebrows, and she wasn't wearing makeup, but her short dress was the latest style and it fit her perfectly. Vera was embarrassed by her faded plaid skirt and scuffed shoes. Her own mother looked dowdy and plain compared to Tantig Anahid.

They were ushered to the balcony where Tantig served tea, Seven Up, and store-bought French cookies arranged on a white plate with a gold rim. The balcony was lined with potted plants and a jasmine vine that spilled over the railing. From there, they had a clear view down into the fenced schoolyard across the street.

Tantig said, "When the children are at recess, I watch them from here. They make such a racket, but I tell myself it's the sound of life, which is what we need right now."

Nora said, "She yells at my brother from up here. He's rotten."

"Don't talk about your brother like that. Viken is a good boy," Tantig said. "He's at his friend's house this afternoon. You'll meet him next time. Sometimes he gets into a little mischief. And the Badveli at the school is very strict. You know how the Protestants are. But it's so close, and with the way things are, I couldn't bear to send them any place else."

Her mother said, "For us, it's closer than any of the other high schools. No bridges, no buses, and no crossing the Green Line."

"Girls," Tantig Anahid said, "we grown-ups need some time to talk. Why don't you go play with dolls?"

"Dolls? We're not babies," Nora said.

"Show her your figurines then. Can you imagine, she has a collection of glass figurines? We wrap them in newspaper, then unwrap them, then wrap them again."

As Vera and Nora walked down the windowless hallway, Nora said, "We sleep on the floor here when the rockets are bad. Sometimes we go to Zahlé where my grandparents live. Their house is big, with a garden, and all my cousins are there. I wish we could live there, but my father's work is in the city. Plus, I love my bedroom."

Nora swept open the bedroom door. The walls were white, the carpet and the bedspreads on the twin beds were pink. The white vanity table had a ruffled pink skirt, and there were white nightstands beside the beds. Vera imagined that if she were to stay overnight, she and Nora would lie in the twin beds, side by side in the dark, talking until they fell asleep. Then she remembered that if she were to stay at Nora's, they would be cowering on the floor in the hall.

On the wall above Nora's desk, there were two shelves of glass figurines. She passed them to Vera to be admired. Among them were a swan, an octopus, a miniature aquarium with three fish, and a porcelain ballerina with a real pink tulle skirt.

"I love this one," Vera said as she held the ballerina.

"That's my favorite," Nora said.

"Where do you get them?" Vera asked.

"When my father goes on a trip, he brings them back. My brother collects Matchbox cars, and that's what my dad gets him. If it's a long trip, he buys jewelry for my mother. And when he goes to Paris, he always buys her perfume."

She paused and looked at Vera expectantly. Vera wasn't sure what to say.

"You're lucky," Vera said finally. "My father never goes anywhere."

Nora said, "Too bad you're not in my grade. I would introduce you to my friends."

Vera understood that Nora would never introduce her to her friends.

"Do you like the school?" Vera asked.

"It's okay. The uniforms are ugly, but I have lots of friends. At chapel every morning, the Badveli reads from the Bible, and we sing a hymn. It's boring, but we pass notes to the boys."

When Vera and her mother departed, they were carrying two shopping sacks filled with school uniforms that Nora had outgrown.

As they descended the stairs, Mairig said, "Now I remember why I never see her. She talks so much I barely could say a word. She didn't ask a single question—not one about you, my mother, anything."

"Nora seemed nice," Vera said.

"Anahid is nice. She will take you when there's a problem, and you can stay for as long as needed. She is generous because it makes her the queen. Did you see those eyebrows? Ridiculous."

The walls of the high-ceilinged chapel were white, and the wood trim was dark. Vera, Taline, and Seta were seated in a pew with the other girls in their class. The boys were in the row behind them, and one of the boys was kicking rhythmically on the wooden back of their pew.

The Badveli told them about his personal friend and savior Jesus Christ. He said that Jesus longed to be their friend as well. Then he said, "Dear children, you must be in this world, but not of it. You must stay on the narrow path that will bring you to the right hand of God. You must avoid the wide road that leads to death and destruction."

Vera knew that the Badveli meant that they should not steal money from the offering box, or smoke cigarettes, or tell lies to their parents, or kiss boys. But the way he said it would be confusing for the smaller children. If they were listening—and from all the fidgeting in the front rows, it wasn't clear that they were—they would be afraid to walk on the avenue, thinking that it was the wide road that the Badveli had said would lead them straight to the fires of hell.

It was a rainy day, and the ceiling of their classroom leaked. Digin Karakashian placed a wastepaper basket beneath the dripping water that plinked and splashed as it landed. That morning there was no electricity, so they gathered around a large lantern in the middle of the room for their first lesson.

The day went by slowly—after studying math, they moved on to Armenian language and history. In the afternoon, they had just started their Arabic class when automatic gunfire stuttered outside the school compound. The Arabic teacher stopped mid-sentence, his head cocked to one side, and the kids froze in place. The shooting continued but sounded farther away, and then a missile shrieked overhead.

The principal made an announcement over the loudspeaker directing them to proceed to the school basement, which served as a makeshift bomb shelter. Digin Karakashian directed them to line up single file by the classroom door, then she led them out into the hall. When another missile whistled overhead, the lines on the stairs broke down into a chaotic rush. In the school's lobby, mothers who lived nearby were waiting with dripping umbrellas. Vera saw Tantig Anahid, who beckoned to her.

"Here, sweetie," she said. "You're coming with us."

Vera glanced at Taline and Seta.

Seta said, "Digin Karakashian is taking us home. My mother arranged it."

Their teacher lived near the school, and she was related to Seta's father in some complicated way that Vera didn't quite understand.

Vera joined Tantig. Nora arrived, and then Viken strolled over with a friend.

"Can Daniel come home with us?" he asked.

"Look," Tantig said, "his mother is calling him."

A missile thudded nearby, shaking the building.

"Hurry, hurry, let's go," Tantig said, grabbing Viken by the hand.

That evening, Vera met Nora's father, who from the minute he walked into the apartment barked orders at his wife and children as though they were his employees. Tantig Anahid told

Vera to call him Hrant Amo, but in her head Vera thought of him as The King.

They crowded into the long, narrow interior hallway, which was lit by two battery-operated lanterns. All of them sat on cushions on the floor, except for Nora's father, who was above them in an armchair with a hassock that took up too much space. Vera imagined him wearing a golden crown and holding a jeweled scepter.

At suppertime, Tantig Anahid went to the kitchen, returning with a tray of sandwiches and a bowl of fruit. She handed out flatware and cloth napkins, then their plates.

"Isn't this fun?" she said. "It's like a picnic."

Nora said, "Ouch! You little jerk. He pinched me."

Viken said, "I did not pinch you."

"You did too, you snake," Nora said.

The King growled, "Enough."

For the rest of the evening, Vera spoke to the adults only in response to direct questions. They spread out the mattresses where they would sleep, and Vera sat on hers, using a flashlight to do her homework.

"What's the point of that?" Nora said. "There won't be school tomorrow."

"How do you know?" Viken said.

"You hear the fighting. Once they get started like that, it means no school for at least a day or two," Nora answered. "Right, Baba?"

The King grunted, "Jackasses."

Vera wasn't sure if he was referring to the fighters outside or to his children.

"Little ones," said Tantig, "please run like rabbits to your rooms and put on your night clothes. Make sure you stay far from the windows."

In her bedroom, Nora pulled a flowered nightgown with lace trim from the drawer. Vera reached for the nightshirt in the bottom of the overnight bag she had left in Nora's closet. As the older girl took off her top and unhooked her bra, Vera quickly turned her back and pulled the nightshirt over her head, using it as a tent under which to unbutton her blouse and undo her own training bra. She had caught a glimpse of Nora's full breasts and was embarrassed about how pitifully small her own were.

When they returned to the hallway, The King had gone down to the lobby to talk with the night watchman. As Nora and Vera settled into bed, Viken flicked small wads of paper at them. One landed in Vera's hair and when it stuck, she realized it was covered in spit. The next one hit Nora's cheek.

"You blockhead!" Nora said.

His response was to throw his pillow at her.

"Mama, tell him to stop, or I will bash his face in," Nora said.

"What way is that to talk about your little brother?" Tantig said.

A spitball flew between Nora and Vera, hitting the wall behind them.

"That's it," Nora said. "Let's go, Vera."

They dragged their mattresses to the other end of the hall, just outside Nora's bedroom.

The King returned, and Tantig put out the lanterns. The hallway was dark. The shelling outside stopped and started repeatedly, but it wasn't close by. There were occasional bursts of gunfire, but they also sounded distant.

Vera heard snoring from the end of the hall where Nora's parents and brother were bedded down. She couldn't tell if Nora was asleep. She wondered about her family in Nor Hadjin. She hoped that Medz Mama had remembered to bring the canary's cage into the house. Vera was the one who usually did that.

"Are you awake?" Nora whispered.

"Yes," she answered.

"If I tell you something," Nora said, "will you promise you won't say anything?"

"Of course," Vera said.

"Not your mother, not your friends, nobody? You promise?"

"I promise."

"You swear on your mother's soul?"

"I swear."

"It's a secret, and I haven't told anyone," she said.

"You can trust me."

It seemed strange that Nora, who barely glanced at Vera in the halls at school, was going to entrust her with such a secret.

"I have a boyfriend," Nora said.

Vera ran through the faces of the eighth and ninth grade boys, trying to imagine which one it might be. Nora was beautiful, and Vera was sure that her boyfriend had to be one of the best-looking ones. There was a boy named Ara in the eighth grade who had the good looks of a movie star.

"Is it Ara?" Vera asked.

"That baby? My boyfriend is much older than that," Nora said.

"Is he in the tenth grade?"

The older girl stifled a laugh. "Not likely."

"A senior?" she asked.

"Older," Nora said.

Vera wanted to know exactly how much older, but instead she asked, "How did you meet him?"

"He works for his father, who is a jeweler. They had a shop in the Souk and lived in Kantari, but because of the war they moved to Ashrafieh. They opened a store not far from Sourp Hagop. One day when I was looking in the shop window with Maro, he invited us to come inside. He was very friendly, and he asked our names. I went back another day by myself, and he showed me a gold bracelet he thought I would like. That's how it started. And now we try to find ways to see each other. It's almost impossible. My mother watches the schoolyard, the gate, and the street, and if anyone saw us together, they would tell her."

"How long have you known him?" Vera asked.

"Three months. And that bracelet he showed me, he gave it to me as a gift, but I can't wear it. If my mother finds out, she will go crazy."

"What's his name?"

"Nareg. Isn't that perfect? Nareg and Nora. Nora and Nareg. He says that he loves me. And the other day, he told me that he wants to marry me."

It was so romantic, like something you would read about in a book or see in a movie. Nora and Nareg would run away together, and a priest would marry them in a small church by the sea. They would have four children, two sets of twins, and give each of them a name that started with the letter N. But something was wrong with this scene. Nora was only fourteen years old. No priest would marry them without her parents' permission and Vera couldn't imagine Tantig and The King saying yes. In fact, they would probably force Nora to live in a convent guarded over by nuns.

Nora said, "I hid the bracelet under my mattress. My mother goes through my dresser drawers and looks in my school bag and coat pockets, but won't think to look there. She's always spying on me. She even reads my diary. So now I write stupid things to put her off track. Sometimes I feel like she can read my mind. When I'm thinking about Nareg, she looks at me suspiciously and says, 'What are you thinking about?' Then I pretend that I have a crush on Ara because my mother believes he would be the perfect boyfriend."

As Nora talked, Vera was relieved she wasn't expected to give advice because she had no experience with boys.

Nora said, "My father is ten years older than my mother. They got married when my mom was eighteen. It shouldn't be a problem that Nareg is older than I am."

Vera wondered exactly how old Nareg was. What if he was thirty? That was more than twice Nora's age.

"Has he ever kissed you?" Vera said. She immediately regretted asking something so personal and she was afraid that Nora would be offended.

But Nora wasn't angry. She said, "Yes. More than once."

Her mother called down the hall, "What are you two whispering about?"

"We're talking about boys," Nora said. She poked Vera and laughed.

Tantig said, "Enough gossiping. Go to sleep."

"Remember what you promised," Nora said. Then she rolled over and turned her face to the door.

Soon they were all asleep, except for Vera, who lay on her back staring up at the ceiling. She thought for a while about Nora's secret romance, imagining Nora in a jewelry shop trying on rings set with glittering diamonds. Then she envisioned her family crouched in the cramped hallway in Nor Hadjin. What if the house had been hit by a rocket? The roof had collapsed, and they were trapped under wooden beams and chunks of plaster. And if they were unharmed, she was sure they were sick with worry about her, especially her grandmother.

Vera dreamed that she was walking through a bombed-out street where stray cats and dogs nosed through the trash looking for food. A storefront was in flames and there were large shards of glass scattered across the sidewalk. Down the street, she saw Nora in the distance. Nora was wearing a floor-length white wedding dress and a white lace veil. She walked hand in hand with Nareg, who looked like Ara except that he was tall, and he had a moustache. Nora held up the hem of her skirt with her free hand as they picked their way through the ruins of wrecked buildings. Nora's mother, her father, and the Badveli raced past Vera. The Badveli shouted, "My girl, you are halfway to ruin! You must turn back!" Nora and Nareg started to run.

It was Sunday, and they had borrowed the old silver Peugeot from their father's friend, Koko the Mechanic. Her parents were in the front seat, and Vera and her brothers in the back, all of them dressed in their church clothes. They were on their way to a birthday party for one of her mother's childhood friends. The drive should have taken fifteen minutes, but instead the traffic crept so slowly that Vera watched as people strolled past on the sidewalk. It was a hot day in late September, uncollected garbage was rotting in piles along the street, and the sun was beating down on the roof.

Their mother fanned herself with the church bulletin and asked, "What's happening? Can you see?"

Their father wiped sweat from his neck with a handkerchief. "I can't see anything."

The line of traffic stalled. Someone behind them honked a horn, and then everyone was honking. The racket was hellish and unrelenting.

Raffi started whining. "Mairig, I don't like this. Why are they making so much noise? Why is it taking so long? When are we going to be there?"

"Raffi," Mairig said, "stop. I have a headache, and you're making it worse."

"They're giving me a headache too," Raffi said. "And my stomach hurts. I think I'm going to throw up."

Mairig snapped open her purse, pulled out three lollipops and passed them back to Vera. "This will make you feel better. Vera, help him with the wrapper."

"I want the orange one," Armen said.

"I want the orange one. That's my favorite," Raffi said.

"Give it to the baby," Armen said. "I'll take the red one."

Raffi said, "I am not a baby."

Vera unwrapped the orange lollipop and handed it to her little brother. She opened the yellow one, and the lemon was sharp on the sides of her tongue.

The line of cars slowly edged forward. As their car neared the intersection, the father grunted, and the mother inhaled sharply. Raffi, the white stick of the lollipop poking from his mouth, stood peering over his mother's shoulder, and Armen craned his head out the window. From her vantage in the middle, Vera could see through the front windshield that several cars beyond them men in green fatigues with rifles were halting traffic. Behind the men, a jeep was turned sideways to block the middle of the avenue. This was called a flying checkpoint. Checkpoints had sprung up all over the city, some of them permanent and some of them temporary.

"It's the Kataeb," Armen said, leaning more of his torso out the window.

"Get yourself back into the car," Mairig snapped. "And, Raffi, sit down."

Baba said, "They're checking papers."

The car ahead of them inched forward, and Vera could see the back of its driver's head, the back of his wife's head, and the tops of the heads of four children crammed into the rear seat. One of the militiamen gestured for the car to stop and put his hand in the window to take the driver's identity card. He flicked the card open, scrutinizing the man. He then handed it to another man in fatigues for inspection. Now the militiaman gestured for the driver to get out of the car.

The driver opened his door and stepped out onto the street.

One of the militiamen used the butt of his rifle to slam the driver to the ground. Another one kicked him in the ribs, and another kicked him in the head. Vera heard his groans, or did she imagine them? She couldn't look away from the scene unfolding in front of them. She wanted someone, anyone, to stop them. She wanted the man to get up and run away. But if he tried to escape, they would probably raise their rifles and fire at him as he ran, hitting him in the head and the back.

There was no escaping the sound of the woman in the front seat of the car as she started to scream. She tried to open the passenger door, but a militiaman forced it shut with his boot. Now the children in the back seat were howling. Their father was on the ground with blood streaming from a gash in his head. Two militiamen grabbed him by the arms, pulled him to his feet, and dragged him away, the three of them disappearing down a side street. A militiaman opened the door to let the woman out of the car. She ran around to the driver's side and got in behind the wheel. They waved her on, and she sped away.

The uniformed men turned toward the Serinossians' car, gesturing for them to advance.

As the car rolled toward the checkpoint, Vera could see that the muscles in her father's forearms were taut as cords as he gripped the steering wheel. Her mother glanced over her shoulder for a second, wordlessly warning them to keep quiet. Her mouth was pulled tight, and her eyes were wide. The boys were silent and still. Vera held her breath, afraid that the slightest movement might enrage the men.

Her father offered his identity card out the window. Vera watched the man's hands as the card was examined and then returned to her father. The militiaman stepped back from the car and waved them forward, gesturing to the car behind them to advance. Vera stared down at her trembling hands. In this way she avoided the sight of the rifles slung over the men's shoulders, the expressions on their faces, and most of all their eyes.

"Thank God," Mairig said. "Is there another way we can take on the way home? I don't want to go through that again."

Her father said, "I can try Mar Louis."

Raffi asked, "Why did they do that to him?"

"They didn't like his name," Baba said.

Raffi asked, "Do you think they were taking him to the doctor?"

Armen said, "He's probably not coming back."

"That's enough. I don't want to hear another word about it," said Mairig.

Vera felt like a great stone was bearing down on her. It was so heavy that it was crushing her ribs.

Armen announced, "She's crying again."

Her mother said, "Vera, that's enough. You don't know that man. He's nothing to you. You can't cry for the whole world."

Vera covered her face with her hands, pressing her palms against her cheeks. She saw the man lying on the ground as they kicked him like a dog. She thought that no one should do that even to a dog. Despite what her mother said, Vera thought to herself, *Yes, it is, it is possible to cry for the whole world.*

On Saturday morning, Vera, her brothers, and her cousin Kevork sat on the curb outside their house. Armen and Kevo were trading marbles while Vera entertained Raffi with puppets that Medz Mama had helped them make out of old socks. Suddenly, they heard the loud crack of what they had come to know as the sound of a sniper's rifle.

Seconds later, Melkon, the boy who delivered the *Ararad* newspaper to families who lived near the bridge, came speeding around the corner on his bicycle. He raced past them, halting in front of Amo Vahram's bike shop.

"I've been hit," Melkon said.

Amo Vahram ran through the door and caught Melkon as he dropped. He pulled the boy off the bike and sat on the curb holding him across his lap. The boy's head wilted onto Amo's shoulder.

"Dear God, Melkon, dear God, my boy," Vahram said. "What have they done to you?"

Raffi cried, "Who did that? Who hurt Melkon?"

Vera pulled Raffi toward her as he sobbed. His small shoulder blades heaved up and down under her hand.

Vera had seen other sniper victims—an abandoned dog fallen in a heap of trash, an old man lying on the bridge with a sack of olives scattered around him, and a woman her mother's age who had been hit while walking on the avenue. Vera couldn't detect any pattern in the killings. Why on this morning had the sniper chosen poor Melkon and not someone else?

Vera's father emerged from his carpentry shop. He glanced

at Melkon and commanded Armen and Kevork, "Boys, run get Dr. Nazo. Vera, take Raffi home now."

Armen sped toward the doctor's office with Kevo at his heels, and Vera pulled Raffi in the opposite direction toward their house.

Raffi asked, "Vera, is Melkon going to die? Have they killed him?"

"Don't worry, Raffi. Dr. Nazo will take care of him," Vera told him.

Their mother took one look at Raffi's tear-streaked face. "What happened?"

"The sniper shot Melkon," Vera said.

Medz Mama moaned, "*Vahkh, vahkh.* Not Melkon. That sweet boy never did anything to anyone."

"I'll be back," Mairig said as she rushed out the door.

Medz Mama sat in her armchair, and Vera and Raffi were on the sofa. The grandmother picked up the lace doily she was knotting, but her hands were unsteady, so she put it down. Raffi climbed into her lap where he sat sucking his thumb and stroking the side of her face with his other hand.

"Tell me a story," he said.

"Ah, my little mouse, I can't think of a story right now," Medz Mama said. "Shall I sing you a song?"

Vera had no idea how long they were waiting. It could have been minutes, or it could have been hours. Again and again, she heard the long echo of the sniper fire and saw Melkon rounding the corner on his bicycle, his legs peddling as quickly as he could. A bright red flower bloomed in the center of his white shirt.

When Armen and their parents returned, Vera knew from the cast of their faces that Melkon had not survived.

"Did Dr. Nazo fix him?" Raffi asked.

Their father said, "No, son. Dr. Nazo tried, but poor Melkon was too badly injured. It wasn't possible to save him."

Soon after the Christmas holiday, Vera was leaving school with Taline and Seta when she saw Nora lingering by the gate. She wondered who Nora was waiting for and was surprised when the older girl fell into step beside them.

"Let me walk you down the hill," Nora said.

Vera knew that Nora wanted something, but that she wouldn't say anything in front of the other girls. As Nora complained about how boring the holiday had been with her family, Vera was interested to see how she would manage to get rid of her friends.

Once they had turned the corner, where Tantig Anahid couldn't see them from the balcony, Nora placed her hand on Vera's forearm and slowed her pace. At the head of the flight of stairs leading down to Mar Mikhael, Nora said to Taline and Seta, "You can go. I want to talk to Vera."

Once they were out of earshot, Nora said, "I need you to do something for me."

Her voice was desperate, and Vera was thrilled. She guessed she was about to be asked to play a small part in the ongoing drama of Nora and Nareg.

Nora pulled a knotted handkerchief from her school bag. "I want you to keep this for me."

"What is it?" Vera asked.

Nora thrust it into Vera's hand. "The gold bracelet. Put it in your bag."

Vera shoved the white hankie into her school satchel.

Nora said, "I had to get it out of the apartment. You take it home, and tomorrow, you will bring it to him in his shop."

"I don't know where that is," Vera said.

"Tomorrow, I'll give you a message for him and the address."

"Did your mother find out?" Vera asked.

"She doesn't know much. When we were in Zahlé for Christmas, Nareg and I missed each other so much. It wasn't even a month, but it felt like a hundred years. His family goes to Bikfaya for the holidays, but he has cousins in Zahlé. He sent a letter for me with his cousin, and I went to his cousin's café to see if there was anything for me. I sat down and answered his letter right there in the café, and his cousin promised to get it to Nareg. I put that letter with his other notes in an old cigar box, and I hid the box in the back of the garden. I should have thrown them away, but his letters were so beautiful."

"Did your mother find them?" Vera asked.

"No," Nora said, shaking her head. "The problem was when Nareg drove to Zahlé. We arranged to meet at the café, but a neighbor saw me and told his wife, and then the old witch told my mother."

"What did your mother do?" Vera asked.

"She asked me how I knew him, and I made up a story. I said it was the first time that I had met him. I said just by chance he sat down at the table next to mine in the café, and we started a conversation."

"Did she tell your father?"

"No. But she didn't believe me. I sneaked out to the garden and ripped the letters into tiny pieces, and then I threw them onto the pile of rubbish my grandfather was burning. I'm never going to forgive her for making me do that. Since we've been back, she goes through my drawers all the time. I saw her on the balcony with opera glasses watching me in the schoolyard. I didn't even know that she had opera glasses. She asks my friends questions and gossips with their mothers. I keep thinking she's going to hire a spy to follow me. She's turning my room upside down."

Just then, Vera glanced up to see Tantig marching toward them.

"There she is," Vera whispered.

Nora rolled her eyes. "She's crazy."

"Oh, there you are," her mother called. "I wondered where you were going. It's nice to see you, Vera. Do you want to come home with us for tea and cookies?"

One glance at Nora's stony face told Vera how to answer.

"Thank you, Tantig, but my mother's expecting me," Vera said.

"Say hello to her from me," Tantig Anahid said. "I haven't seen her in months. Tell her she should come by for coffee some afternoon."

"I will, Tantig. See you tomorrow, Nora." Vera turned and ran down the steps.

As Vera sat at the kitchen table after supper with Armen doing homework, the hankie was in the bottom of the bag at her feet. Vera imagined her mother rooting around in the satchel, something her mother never did. Finding the handkerchief, she would untie the knot and discover the bracelet.

"Where did you get this?" her mother would ask.

And what would Vera say? She couldn't tell her that it was Nora's. She would have to make up an elaborate lie, and unlike Nora, Vera was a terrible liar.

At the end of the school day, Vera saw that Nora was lurking next to the gate. She leaned against the wall, wedged into a corner where her mother wouldn't be able to see her from the balcony, with or without opera glasses.

"You brought it?" Nora asked.

Vera nodded.

Nora handed Vera an envelope addressed to Nareg, along with a slip of paper with the name of the shop, and a small hand-drawn map with the route from the school to the shop. Nora traced her finger on the map, indicating the path, mentioning landmarks along the way. It was about ten minutes from the school.

Nora said, "Wait here for a couple of minutes until I get upstairs. I don't want my mother to see you going in that direction. When I get home, I'll make sure she isn't on the balcony. And then you can go."

"How will I know which one is Nareg?" Vera asked.

"At this hour, he will be the only one in the shop."

Vera watched Nora cross the street and enter the vestibule of her building. Then Vera envisioned Nora ascending the four flights of stairs. When she guessed that Nora had reached her apartment, she counted slowly to one hundred. She looked up at the balcony and saw that Tantig was not at her usual spot on the balcony. Then she ran.

Vera was out of breath when she arrived in front of Zakarian Bijouterie. She peered past the jeweled necklaces, earrings, and bracelets in the display window but didn't see anyone inside. As she opened the door, a bell jangled, and a man emerged from a back room. He approached and stood behind the glass showcase.

In Vera's mind Nareg was an older version of Ara the Handsome. Like Ara, Nareg would be tall and slim, with a perfectly symmetrical face and shiny black hair. As she walked toward the counter staring at the man ahead of her, Vera decided that the only quality Nareg shared with Ara was the black hair. Although Nareg's face was slightly crooked, he was still good-looking enough—he resembled Adiss, the pop singer Vera's mother loved. Both Nareg and Adiss had moustaches, goatees, and crescent-shaped eyebrows. But there was a roll of fat resting on the top of Nareg's belt, and once she reached the counter, Vera noticed that there were tufts of hair on his knuckles, and he had long, bushy sideburns. Vera couldn't tell exactly how old he was, but he was much too old and hairy for Nora.

"May I help you, sweetheart?" he asked.

"Nareg?" Vera said.

"Yes, that's me." His moustache was like a centipede crawling above his lip.

"Nora asked me to bring this to you." She slid the hankie and the letter across the glass countertop.

He tore open the envelope and read the note. He unknotted the fabric and palmed the bracelet, which he dropped into his shirt pocket. He folded the note and slid that into his pocket as well.

"I want to send her a message. Can you wait?" he asked.

"My mother is going to worry if I'm not home soon."

"Two minutes, I promise."

He scribbled on a scrap of paper, tucked it into an envelope, and licked the flap to seal it. As he handed Vera the envelope, he eyed her as though noticing her for the first time.

"Are you Nora's friend?" he asked.

"My mother and her mother are cousins," Vera said.

"Do you go to school together?" he asked.

"Yes. But we're not in the same grade," she said.

"When you grow up, you are going to be a real heartbreaker." He winked at her.

"I have to go now," Vera said as she backed away from the counter.

Nareg smiled, his teeth flashing beneath his moustache. "And you're not going to say a word to your mother, are you, *joudig*?"

After the Sunday service, Vera lingered near her parents and the other adults outside the church. They were staring up at a pillar of black clouds rising above Karantina, a neighborhood that had once bordered Hadjin but was now on the other side of the highway. The air was heavy with wood smoke and the smell of burning gasoline.

Hadjinian the Jeweler said, "The Kataeb told us to get our people out before the cleansing operation. It will be finished by tomorrow."

"And is everyone out?" her father asked.

"Maybe we missed a few. But they promised they wouldn't touch them," Hadjinian said.

Her mother said, "You trust those scoundrels? Do you imagine them saying, 'Armenians to one side, Palestinians and Muslims to the other, if you please'?"

Noticing Vera at her elbow, Mairig said, "Miss Big Ears, go play with the other girls."

Vera approached Taline, who was watching the boys kick a soccer ball around on the street in front of the church compound. Taline's twin brothers raced toward the ball, bumping into each other and tumbling to the ground.

Taline said, "If they wreck their Sunday suits, my mother is going to beat them."

"Did you see the smoke over Karantina?" Vera asked.

Taline said, "My grandparents are there. My father couldn't get them on the phone last night. He drove over this morning, but they weren't letting anyone in."

Just then the stuttering of automatic weapons could be heard from afar. Vera flinched at the sound of distant shouts and a woman's scream. Armen picked up the soccer ball, and the boys came to stand near the girls. There was a staccato burst of gunfire, this time sounding closer.

Armen said, "Kalashnikovs."

The next morning as Vera met up with Taline and Seta for the walk to school, Dr. Nazo rushed past them toward the church. He was carrying his black leather medical bag.

"Good morning, girls!" he called.

As they neared the avenue, Vera saw a woman carrying an injured toddler walking toward them. The little girl had a blood-stained cloth wound around her head. The mother's face was darkened with soot and there were streaks where tears had run down her cheeks.

Vera asked Taline, "What happened to your grandparents?"

She said, "My father went to Karantina early this morning and brought them to our house. Yesterday they hid in their bathroom the whole day."

Once the mother and child were out of sight, Taline continued, "My father told us there were dead bodies all over the place. They killed people in the streets and threw them into the river. They nailed people to the front doors of their houses. They set houses on fire. They left my grandparents' house alone, but I don't think they'll ever be able to go back there to live."

Seta said, "My dad said that Dr. Nazo is setting up an infirmary in the school. There were so many people coming to his office for help last night, he didn't have room for them. They were lined up on the street."

Taline continued, "My grandmother was saying things that

don't make any sense. My father and my grandfather didn't know what to do, so my father went to get Der Hayr."

On the avenue Vera saw two more wounded men trudging toward Nor Hadjin. Their faces were smudged, and their clothes were grimy and stained with dried blood. Vera tried not to stare, but one man had a gaping cut in his cheek, and the other had a bloodied shirt wrapped around his hand.

When Vera arrived home from school in the afternoon, her grandmother and Raffi were standing by as her mother hurriedly gathered an armful of old bedsheets.

"I'm helping Dr. Nazo in the infirmary," Mairig said as she headed for the door. "They need more bandages. Go let your father know I will be home late."

Vera's father wasn't in his shop. Amo Vahram, who was repairing a bicycle next door, told Vera that her father and Armen had gone to Karantina.

"They went with Garo Sahakian to check on his furniture factory," he said.

Vera sat at the kitchen table with her books and notebooks spread out in front of her while the grandmother worked at the stove. Raffi stood on a chair wearing one of their grandmother's aprons stirring onions in the pan with a wooden spoon.

Vera ran her eyes over the same sentence repeatedly and couldn't remember what she had just read. Her mind was filled with Karantina, the smoke, the cries they had heard the day before, and the injured people streaming into the neighborhood that morning. The father of the little girl with the bloody bandage had probably been murdered. Vera didn't want to be a human if this was the kind of thing that humans did to each other. She didn't want to be an animal that hunted or was hunted. Maybe she could be a tortoise on a remote island in the Pacific Ocean. She had read that a tortoise eats grass and leaves and can live to be a hundred years old, although Vera was not sure it would be a good idea to live that long.

When Baba and Armen arrived, Vera cleared her books and set the table for dinner. The serving bowls were passed in silence. They had taken only a few bites when Mairig rushed in.

She slumped into her chair. "Dr. Nazo is treating a man who is burned like shish kebab from head to foot..." She glanced at Raffi's face and stopped.

Medz Mama slid a plate of food across the table toward her daughter-in-law. "Eat," she said, as though food could fix anything.

Vera placed her fork on the table, feeling queasy.

Mairig said, "By the end, there were eight of us helping Nurse Kohar and the doctor. More volunteers arrived just now, so I could leave. Dr. Nazo said he will give us first aid classes. I'll have some skills for the next time."

Baba said, "Araxi, may there never be a next time. We drove to Karantina with Garo to see about his factory. He was lucky. They looted, but they didn't burn it down. We also stopped by the flourmill. People fled there with the Kataeb chasing right behind them. Some of them crawled into the milling machines to hide, but that didn't save them. They slaughtered them like sheep."

Vera wished her father would stop talking.

Her mother asked, "We? You and Garo and who else?"

"Garo's boy and Armen," her father answered.

Mairig said, "Have you lost your mind? You took your son to see a massacre?"

"Garo's boy was going, and Armen wanted to go too," Baba said.

Her mother's voice rose. "And if he told you he wanted to go to hell, would you take him there? Your son's face looks like he has seen twenty demons, a *dev*, and Satan himself."

"I don't want you to talk about me. I didn't see anything, you hear me. I saw nothing at all," Armen shouted. He leaped up from the table, knocking over the chair as he bolted from the room.

As Vera swept the floor in her father's shop, two Lebanese youths, dressed in fatigues with rifles on straps slung over their shoulders, came through the shop door. With the broom in her hand, she edged backward toward her father, who switched off the lathe.

The tall, clean-shaven one, who had a small oval birthmark on his cheek, said in Arabic, "Good afternoon, sir. Now that we are providing protection for your neighborhood, we have come to collect a voluntary contribution."

The short one with curly hair and a beard that looked like small clumps of cooked spinach thrust a piece of paper toward her father, saying, "Here's your receipt, sir."

He examined the paper, his lips pressed into a grim line. Vera understood that there was no way for Baba to refuse them no matter what number they had written on the paper.

Her grip on the broom handle tightened, and she glanced at the faded black and white picture of Medzn Mourad, one of the heroes of the defense of Hadjin, tacked to the wall above her father's workbench. The *fedayi* wore a black hat with no brim and a dark jacket with belts full of bullets crisscrossed over his chest and wrapped around his waist. Staring into the distance, he was holding an ancient rifle. They needed Mourad now. She wished that she could use the broom to sweep these two out onto the street like so much rubbish.

Her father reached for the metal cash box, counted out some bills, stuffed them into an envelope and held it out.

"Thank you, sir," the tall one said, pocketing the envelope.

"We will come collect your contribution each month," Spinach Face said.

When Vera observed them turn into her uncle's bicycle shop next door, she wanted to shout at them, but fear constricted her throat.

"Are they going into all the shops?" she asked her father.

"Apparently. Extortion seems to be their new business," he said. "Don't think about those bandits anymore, my girl, what's done is done."

"But they'll be back," she said.

He shrugged and leaned toward the lathe, flipping on the switch.

"A bullet can go through one wall," Armen explained to Vera and Raffi, "and sometimes two, but no bullet can make it through three walls. It's good to be on the ground floor so if a missile hits the house it would have to break through the roof and the second floor to get us. The hallway is the safest place because there are no windows, it's on the ground floor, and there are two walls between us and the street."

Raffi clasped and unclasped his fingers as his eyes darted from side to side. Vera could tell he was trying not to cry.

"You're not helping," Vera said to Armen.

Later that night as the ground rocked and the windows shattered, they were crammed together in the candlelit hallway of their house. Raffi curled into a ball on couch cushions in the farthest, darkest corner. Medz Mama sat beside him, whispering into his ear and rubbing circles on his back. Vera sat with her spine pressed against the wall with her jaw clenched so tightly that it gave her a headache. It sounded as though elephants were rampaging outside and that at any moment they might crash through the wall in a mad stampede. Vera and her family would be trampled underfoot, their house flattened, its beams splintered.

"Are we going to die?" Raffi asked. "I don't want to die."

Baba said, "We aren't going to die, little mouse. It will be morning soon and they will stop."

Mairig said, "What kind of hell is this? I don't know who I hate more, Gemayel or Jumblatt."

"You can hate them both the same," he answered.

"Come over here with Raffi and me, Vera and Armen." Their grandmother beckoned to them. "I will tell you a story."

Vera felt too old for her grandmother's tales about magic animals, giants, witches, and maidens. On the other hand, what else was there to do? Just then Vera noticed that it was quiet. There was a lull in the shelling, and she hoped they were done for the night.

"What kind of story do you want?" Medz Mama asked.

"Tell us the one about the evil *dev* who blocked the fountains so there was no water to drink and then he ran around kidnapping the goats and munching on their bones," Armen said.

"That's too scary," said Raffi.

Armen said, "Yeah, but the *dev* gets his head chopped off in the end."

"I don't like that part either," Raffi said.

"Why don't you tell us a Sosi story," Vera said.

"That's good," said Raffi.

Their grandmother took a breath, and then she started with the traditional opening to an Armenian tale, *"Gar ou chigar*...There was and there was not in the mountain town of Hadjin a girl named Sosi."

Raffi said, "And Sosi understood what the birds were saying..."

"That's right, my little one, she talked with the birds," Medz Mama said. "But tonight, I have a new story for you about a fox who was her friend. This swift and clever fox built its den under a stone wall at the edge of the orchard..."

The next evening at dinner their father told them about a bomb shelter that the local committee was preparing.

"It's in the underground garage of the six-story building up the hill," he said.

Mairig added, "I bought a small suitcase for each of you. Choose your special toys, and put them in with a change of clothes, a toothbrush, and so on."

Their father said, "We will leave them by the front door so if we have to go in a hurry, they will be ready."

Vera and her brothers sorted through their belongings, putting in essentials and leaving less important items to one side. Raffi packed his collection of plastic trolls, an old satin slip of his mother's that he often wrapped around his shoulders at night, a small stuffed bear, his Sunday shoes, and several pairs of socks. Armen filled his suitcase with an assortment of comic books, lead toy soldiers that had belonged to their father, and the drawstring cloth bag that held his marbles.

Certain that a direct hit from a rocket or a shell would turn to ash any papers they left behind, Vera gathered family photographs, some of them loose snapshots, one a studio portrait in a frame, and a small photo album. Her grandmother had used black photo corners to carefully arrange pictures in the album that spanned from the building of their house in Nor Hadjin in the 1930s to Raffi's fifth birthday party. Vera included her school reports, added a tin of colored pencils and a sketchbook, and finally crammed in the two blonde plastic lady dolls that she was embarrassed to admit she still adored.

Their father gave each of them a flashlight and spare batteries. The grandmother contributed chocolate bars and bags of roasted almonds. Their mother added packets of tissues and plastic hair combs.

Word spread through the neighborhood that something big was about to happen. With his ear pressed to his battery-operated transistor, Baba listened to the news and tried to puzzle out what might soon be bearing down on them.

"I can't tell what's going on," he said. "Maybe the rumors are true. We'll see what the night brings."

When the shelling started, it was heavier than ever before. Their parents roused them from their beds and hurried them downstairs. They picked up their suitcases, and Vera carried Shakar's cage in her other hand.

"You are going to bring that cage with us?" her mother asked.

"We can't leave him here," Vera said.

"He is part of our family," Raffi said.

Their mother rolled her eyes and sighed.

Medz Mama and Raffi, who were the slowest, walked in front, and Mairig was just behind urging them on. Their father brought up the rear with cushions slung over his shoulder as they filed toward the garage. Kevo ran up and fell into step with Armen as they turned from their street onto the avenue.

"Where are your parents?" Mairig asked him.

"They're coming. I ran ahead when I saw you."

As they approached a heavily sandbagged checkpoint on the avenue, the Kataeb militiamen waved them through. They turned right into a dead-end street that led to the mouth of the garage. Their neighbors filed in behind them, each family setting up a space for itself in the shelter.

Vera hated the place immediately—it smelled of motor oil, axle grease, and mildew; it was dark and damp; and the flashlights and candles cast long shadows that made everything more eerie. Vera remembered one of her grandmother's stories about a dragon that lived in a cave deep in the mountains. The dragon ate anyone who wandered by and kept a princess chained to a rock at the back of the cave. A brave young prince aided by a talking horse finally beheaded the dragon and saved the princess. Now Vera and her family were trapped in a cave and the dragons were outside. But there was no prince to save them.

The first level of the garage served as a car repair shop in the daytime, hence the slick spots of oil and grease on the concrete floor. This was where the families had spread out their bedding. When Vera and Raffi needed to use the bathroom, their mother led the way with a flashlight. They walked down a steep ramp leading to the next level, where there were pails to use for toilets. Vera and Raffi did what they needed to do as quickly as possible. Their mother handed them tissues, then wipes for their hands, and they scurried back to the first level.

Raffi said to Armen, "It stinks and it's really creepy down there."

Armen said, "If you think that's creepy you should see the level below that."

"How do you know?" Vera asked.

"Kevo and I came here yesterday. We went to the bottom. There are abandoned cars and old tires, and we heard rats running around."

Inside the garage there were rodents and the smell of the sour sweat of frightened people. Outside there were men with weapons who were trying to murder each other, and they didn't care who else they might kill in the process.

Vera didn't want to keep thinking about all the horrible ways that they could die. At least she wasn't stuck in the windowless hallway in her house with only her immediate family. Half the neighborhood was here. She went to find Seta and Taline in the far corner where Taline's family had set up.

Taline had brought the treasured Francie doll that her father had special ordered as a birthday gift before the war. Vera coveted that doll, its thick dark hair, rooted eyelashes, and the red-and-white checked minidress. They lined up the dolls along the wall and spread out their outfits, among them several dresses that had been crocheted by Vera's grandmother.

"This is boring," Taline said. "Let's go see what the boys are doing."

The girls approached the far corner where Armen, Kevo, Taline's twin brothers, and some other boys were gathered.

"Where did you get it?" one of the boys asked.

Armen said, "It was on the train bridge."

"What is that, Armen?" Vera asked, poking her head into the circle.

Kevo said, "A grenade."

Armen said, "You girls better clear out. It's a live one."

Seta said, "You are completely crazy."

Sako said, "It's not your business. Nobody invited you. Get your big noses out of here. Go back to where you came from."

Stepan echoed his twin, "Yeah. Get lost."

Taline said, "Listen, you little idiot, don't tell us what to do. You could blow us all up with that."

Armen said, "I'd have to pull the pin, and why would I do that?"

Vera said, "This is the stupidest thing you have ever done."

Armen ignored her. He swaddled the grenade in a piece of old flannel.

"If you don't get rid of that thing the minute we get out of here, I'm going to tell her," Vera said.

Kevo said, "Why do girls always have to ruin everything?"

"Vera, Armen, Kevork," their mother called. "Come here. It's late."

Seta's mother called her next, and soon all the mothers were calling. The kids dragged their shoes over the cement floor and flung themselves on their cushions and mattresses.

Once the flashlights and candles were out, the sounds of the fighting seemed louder and closer. Vera, Armen, Kevo, and Raffi lay side by side, and their grandmother draped a blanket over them. Raffi, who was next to Vera, put one palm on her cheek, and his other thumb went into his mouth. The grandmother started to tell them a story about a magic fish. But the shelling and the shuddering of the ground made it hard to hear or to concentrate. Medz Mama finally gave up and stretched out next to them on the mattress. She hummed an old lullaby. Vera's eyelids felt heavy and the last thing she thought was, *Sleep is a sweet nest.*

In the middle of the day, the principal announced over the loudspeaker that school was shutting down, and they should gather their belongings and go home. School had resumed only a few days earlier after a prolonged lull in the fighting, but Vera could hear the telltale clatter of automatic weapons outside. She tossed notebooks, textbooks, and pencils into her satchel. Once she and her classmates were lined up against the wall, the teacher led them down the stairs. Suddenly, an explosion shook the building, shattering some of the windows, and the orderly descent became a mad scramble.

Vera stood by the gate as the schoolyard emptied, not sure what to do. She didn't think she should attempt to run home while shells were flying, but she wondered if Nora had left without her. Another missile whistled overhead. Just then, she saw Nora approaching with her brother in tow.

"Come on," Nora said. "I had to find this jackass. He was playing around with his stupid friends."

"You're the stupid jackass," Viken said.

As they continued bickering, Vera followed them across the street, into their building, and up the stairs. Viken wanted Nora to carry his book bag and she refused.

"Do you think he was born this lazy, or is it my mother's fault?" Nora called back to Vera.

He twisted around on the stairs, glared at Vera, and said, "What about you? Why don't you do something useful and carry my bag?"

"Ignore him," Nora said. "Let's run."

She sprinted up the stairs, and Vera chased behind her.

"Not fair," Viken shouted. "Wait for me."

Tantig opened the apartment door, beckoning them in. "Hurry, hurry, come inside. My God, they have started, and it isn't even dark yet. Four days ago, I unwrapped the figurines and brought the vases and mirrors out of the closet. Now I had to put them all away again. It makes me want to take a hammer and smash everything myself. Your father got here a few minutes ago. He closed the shutters, and he's taping the windows. He heard on the radio that the Syrians are fighting with the Tigers and the Kataeb in Sodeco. I've filled the sinks, the bathtub, and some pots in the kitchen. Vera, thank God, I was able to get through to your mother on the telephone."

That night when Vera and Nora were lying on mattresses at the end of the hall near the closed bedroom door, they barely spoke to each other. Shells thudded into buildings, and missiles shrieked overhead. Viken whimpered with his head buried in his mother's shoulder. The King cursed the Kataeb, the Tigers, the Israelis, the Palestinians, the Syrians, the Americans, the Russians, and the Turks. Then he blasted individuals, starting with Gemayel, Chamoun, Jumblatt, Assad, Arafat, Begin, and Sadat.

Vera had no idea how bad the shelling was in Nor Hadjin, and if her family was in their house or if they had gone to the shelter, or even if they were still alive. What if she was already an orphan? She would dress in black and go stay with her mother's family in Bourj Hammoud. What if Bourj Hammoud was also under attack? She lay on her back in the dark with tears silently sliding down the sides of her cheeks and into the wells of her ears.

When the shelling paused for a few hours near dawn, they fell asleep. School was canceled. There was no electricity. The telephone line was dead. The water wasn't running. They were in the hallway together the whole next day. The Minassians now had three battery-operated lamps, plus an assortment of flashlights.

The King held the transistor radio up to his ear the way Vera's father did. Tantig sat near one of the lamps and applied makeup while peering into a hand mirror. It seemed strange to be putting on lipstick and eyeliner while hiding in a dark hallway, but Tantig, who saw Vera watching her, explained, "Wearing makeup helps a woman feel a little less desperate."

Later Nora and her mother flipped through fashion magazines while Viken read Asterix comics. Vera pulled out a notebook and sketched portraits of her extended family, as well as of Seta and Taline. Next, she drew scenes from her grandmother's story about Sosi and the clever fox. Vera imagined that her grandmother was at that very moment telling the boys a story. Maybe it was a new story that she had never told before, and Vera was missing it.

Tantig served sandwiches in the hallway. Nora and Viken bickered, and their father shouted at them to stop. Then they napped. Outside there was occasional shelling punctuated by the rapid fire of automatic weapons. They ate a cold supper in the hallway. Vera and Nora carried the dirty dishes to the kitchen and piled them in the sink before rushing back to the hall.

That night the shelling wasn't as close or as loud, and they were all exhausted from the night before, so they shut the flashlights and lamps off early. After Tantig, The King, and Viken were asleep, Nora rolled toward Vera in the dark and said, just above a whisper, "Are you awake?"

"Yes," Vera said.

"If I tell you something, you promise you won't tell anyone."

Vera said, "You know you can trust me."

"My parents are planning to move to Paris at the end of the school year," Nora said. "My dad thinks the war is going to get worse. He says Zahlé isn't going to be safe either. They're moving my grandparents to Anjar. Eventually, they want to bring the whole family to Paris. If they wanted to move to France, they should have had us study French, don't you think? I mean, my French isn't terrible, but after all those years at the Protestant school, my English is better. Anyway, I've decided I'm not going with them."

"You want to stay here by yourself?" Vera asked.

Nora said, "I'm going to Los Angeles with Nareg."

"When is Nareg moving to Los Angeles?"

"We're not sure exactly when. His cousin is already there. And his father wants him to set up a branch of the family business."

"Do your parents know?"

She laughed. "Are you crazy?"

Vera asked, "Do you talk to your friends about this?"

Nora said, "No. I'm afraid they would tell their mothers, and then my mother would find out."

From the other end of the hall, Tantig said, "What are you girls talking about? Go to sleep."

Just then there was a thunderous thud and the building quaked. A shell had landed somewhere nearby. Viken started sniveling. Tantig sat up and turned on one of the lamps. The King cursed the Syrians.

Tantig said, "Well, that's it for sleep tonight. Nora, go find a deck of cards."

The next afternoon, the neighborhood was quiet, and when Nora and Vera went to the balcony, they saw that people had begun to creep out of their buildings, picking their way around the debris. The corner market had opened its metal roll-down gate. Tantig Anahid suggested that Nora and Vera go down to see what they could find on the shelves.

"Get some cheese and crackers, and anything else that looks good," she told them.

Vera realized that this was her chance to make her way home. The fighting might resume soon, but the pause would likely last until evening. She needed less than a quarter of an hour to get to Hadjin.

When Vera told Tantig Anahid that she wanted to go home, the woman started wringing her hands in the same way Medz Mama did. Then, making another familiar gesture, she widened her eyes and pressed her palms to her face.

Tantig said, "If anything happens to you, your mother will never forgive me. I will never forgive myself. God will never forgive me."

The King said, "Calm down, Anahid. They aren't going to start again before nightfall. Think of how worried her mother must be."

"Your poor mother," she said to Vera. "I would lose my mind if my kids weren't with me."

Vera leaped like a rabbit down the long flights of stairs, turning right and left and right again on back streets until she reached the avenue. When she barreled through the front door, her grandmother fell on her and held her face in her hands as though Vera had returned from the dead.

"Thank God, thank God," Medz Mama said. "You're back. My dear girl is here. Jesus heard my prayers."

Mairig snapped, "While you have Jesus's ear, why don't you tell him to rain down fire on the blockheads who are ruining our lives with their fighting."

"What kind of thing is that to say?" her grandmother asked.

"Those Protestant missionaries at the orphanage rotted your mind," Mairig told her.

Vera winced. Raffi burst into tears, and then Armen yelled that they should all shut up. Baba arrived back from his shop into the middle of this scene.

"Enough of this fighting, all of you. The important thing is that our girl is home," he said. "Let's get supper on the table before the fireworks begin for the night."

In the school lobby, at the end of their first day back, Seta said, "She's looking for you." She gestured with her eyes and head toward Nora, who was navigating through the crowd.

"See you later," Taline said.

By the time Nora reached her, Vera was alone.

"I need you to bring a message to Nareg," Nora said.

Vera said, "I don't want to do that."

"Be nice. It will take you twenty minutes. And I'll give you a little something as a reward."

"What kind of reward?" Vera asked.

"I don't know. Let me think about it. I'll bring it for you tomorrow."

Vera put her hand out for the envelope.

Nora brightened. "Merci."

On the way to the jewelry shop, Vera saw that a new checkpoint had been set up near the building with a large Kataeb cedar on its facade. As she passed by, one of the guys at the checkpoint called, "Miss, miss!"

She turned, expecting to see a young woman behind her, but there were only two old men standing on the sidewalk talking.

The guy waved her closer.

"Do you remember me?" he said.

She glanced down at his dusty black boots. She raised her eyes and saw that he wore a small white scarf knotted at his throat and a gold cross on a chain. Then she recognized the oval birthmark on his cheek. It was one of the guys who had come to extort money from her father.

She didn't even try to keep the annoyance out of her voice. "Where's your short friend with the scruffy beard?"

He said, "He was killed by a sniper."

Vera thought immediately of Melkon, and now poor Spinach Face. She said, "That's terrible. I'm so sorry."

"Please don't hold it against me that I collected money from your father. It was my job. Someone else does it now. My name is Michel," he said.

"I have to go," she said.

"What's your name?" he called after her.

She decided she would take side streets so she could avoid the checkpoint on the return trip.

When she reached Nareg's shop, she slapped the envelope on the counter and said, "I don't have much time to wait around."

"Why are you so grumpy? You're much prettier when you smile," he said as he tore open the letter.

He tugged on his moustache as he perused it and grimaced when he finished. He reached for a pen and scribbled a reply. He shoved it into an envelope, licking the seal and pressing it closed.

The next morning after chapel, Vera handed Nora the letter, and asked, "Did you bring me the little something?"

Nora was too engrossed with the note to respond. Vera didn't think she had even heard her.

"Can you come home with me after school?" Nora asked. "I need you to bring something to Nareg."

Tantig wanted them to join her on the balcony for tea, but Nora said they didn't have the time for that. She said that

Vera was in a rush. Nora led Vera to her bedroom and shut the door behind them.

There was a big baby doll with blond curly hair sitting in a rocking chair with some stuffed animals. Nora grabbed the doll, twisted off its head, and extracted a black velvet ring box.

"Put this in your bag," she instructed Vera. "And here's the note."

"And what are you giving me?" Vera asked.

"What do you mean?" Nora said.

"You told me you were going to give me something as a reward for my running back and forth like a messenger girl," Vera replied.

"Do you want me to ask him to give you a piece of jewelry?"

"Not that," Vera said. "My mother would be suspicious."

"Well, what do you want?" Nora asked.

"That," Vera said, pointing to the porcelain ballerina on the shelf.

"Are you kidding?" Nora said.

She shrugged. "You can go yourself."

Nora teared up. "You don't understand how hard this is for me. My mother's like a cat outside a mouse hole. I can't move an inch."

If Nora had for one second treated Vera as a friend, or even as a real person, Vera might have relented. But she resented the way Nora ordered her around and then ignored her in the halls at school. And this resentment called forth a stubbornness Vera hadn't realized that she possessed.

"If you can't move an inch, maybe you should ask one of your friends to go," Vera said.

"Take it," Nora said, grabbing the figurine from the shelf and thrusting it at Vera.

As she walked, Vera wondered about the crisis between Nora and Nareg. She wished she could steam open the envelope and read it. But instead, she pulled out the ring box, snapping open its lid. Inside was what Vera had suspected: a diamond engagement ring. The sparkling stone was the size of a dried chickpea. She shoved the case back in her bag and hurried forward. She felt pleased with herself for thinking of the ballerina, which was wrapped in her sweater and wedged in the satchel. If her mother saw it, she would tell her that Nora had given it to her as a gift.

Michel was at the checkpoint, but Vera skirted around him.

"Can't you stop for a minute?" he said.

"I'm in a rush," she called over her shoulder. "On the way back."

She dropped the velvet box and the note on the counter in front of Nareg.

He quickly flipped the jewel case open and closed. After reading Nora's note he muttered, "Damn your eyes."

"Do you want me to wait?" Vera asked.

"No. You can go," he said, dismissing her with a flick of his wrist.

As the bell jangled over the door on her way out, Vera resolved she would never return to this shop again.

At the checkpoint, Michel said, "So now you will tell me your name?"

"Vera," she said.

"I'm on duty, but I can take a short break. Let's step around the corner for a few minutes to have a cigarette."

Feeling newly emboldened, Vera decided to trail him into the alley. He lit a cigarette and handed it to her, and then lit another one for himself. She inhaled the tiniest amount of smoke, suppressing a cough.

Michel laughed. "You're doing better than I thought."

It was stupid of her to follow this Lebanese militia guy into an alley to have a cigarette with him. But his dark eyes were fixed on her in a way that excited her.

She dropped the cigarette, grinding it into the pavement with the toe of her shoe the way she had seen it done in the movies. "It's late."

"You're leaving already? Don't you like me?"

"I don't know," she said. "You're not Armenian, and you're too old for me."

"Give me a chance. I'm a nice guy," he said. "You'll see."

Vera didn't see Nora at chapel, or in the lobby or the schoolyard. She sought out Maro, who was one of Nora's closest friends.

Maro said, "Ask her brother."

At the end of the school day, Vera waited for Viken by the gate.

"Viken," she called, as she saw him nearing.

He scowled at her. "What do you want?"

"Where's your sister?"

"Her? She took a ferry to Cyprus. And from there she's flying to Los Angeles with that fat old fool."

"What?" She was stunned to hear that Nora had left the country.

"You knew that dirty old man was her boyfriend, didn't you?"

She said, "Maybe."

"They got married at Sourp Hagop," he told her. "Don't feel bad you weren't invited. It was only the priest, the four of us, that guy, and his parents. My mother was crying the whole time."

"I can't believe they let her get married," Vera said.

He eyed her. "You didn't know?"

"Know what?"

"The way you two were always whispering, I thought she must have told you. You better not open your trap. It's the big family shame."

"I won't tell anyone."

"Especially not your mother," Viken warned.

"Don't worry. I can keep a secret."

"The only reason they let her get married was because she's going to have a baby. They didn't tell me, but with all the yelling that went on, I figured it out."

Vera had not liked Nareg's wolfish smile, and now she positively loathed him. She and Viken had at least that in common.

Viken said, "I think my father should have shot the two of them. Bang, bang. But my dad doesn't even own a gun. And tell me, in times like these, what use is a man without a gun?"

"You really are a fool," she said.

"I hate you too," he said. "We're moving to Paris soon, and I won't have to look at your ugly face ever again."

When Vera told her mother that Nora was married and had moved to Los Angeles, she assumed her mother would be shocked. But all her mother said was, "Better that she is alive in California."

It made Vera wonder if her mother would consider marrying her off too if the opportunity arose.

A few days before Tantig Anahid left for Paris, Vera and her mother went to say goodbye. The furniture was covered with sheets, the mirrors and framed pictures were off the walls and wrapped.

Anahid said, "Whenever they stop fighting, I think the war is over, and things will go back to normal. Right now, it feels like maybe we made it through alive without losing our minds. But Berj says it's not over. He's sure it's going to get worse. The quiet might last for a week, or a month, or maybe even two. I don't want to leave Beirut, but we can't take any more of this. Life just isn't possible here anymore."

Vera wondered if Tantig thought for even a second about how that would sound to people who weren't going anywhere. Her mother was silent.

"We heard from Nora," Tantig said. "Now she's complaining that she misses me. She's lonely. She doesn't know anyone in California except for Nareg. What can I say? She's the one who decided to get married and move halfway around the world. They could have come to Paris with us, but no, Nareg insisted that they go to Los Angeles."

As Vera and her mother were about to leave, Anahid gave them two shopping bags filled with the rest of Nora's school uniforms, enough to last Vera through high school if she didn't get plump or grow unusually tall. Anahid also handed Vera the keys to the apartment.

Anahid said, "If you need a place to stay, sweetie, you can still come here. Maybe you could do us a favor and pass by once a week to make sure there aren't squatters or other kinds of trouble. I gave the plants to our neighbor, so there's nothing to water. But if you see some strangers on the balcony, you let your mother know, and she will get in touch with my brother. Who knows? We may be back in the autumn."

In the middle of supper, Baba said, "There's a big fight brewing between the Kataeb and the Syrians. It could be the worst we have seen so far. The committee recommends that we move to the shelter or leave for the countryside. We'll go to the garage tonight."

Vera asked, "How long we will have to be there?"

Her father said, "Nobody knows, but we should plan for five days."

"Five days?" Mairig said. "In that filthy garage? Are you crazy?"

Baba shrugged. "Do you have a better idea?"

Medz Mama said, "*Aman, vahhk, vahkh,* Satan never sleeps."

After the meal, their father moved through the house closing shutters, setting windows ajar, and taping thick plastic sheeting over them on the inside. They had replaced the windowpanes several times since the war had started and would likely have to do it again. Vera watered the plants on the roof and helped her mother shroud the furniture with sheets. Her grandmother was in the kitchen wrapping dishes and glassware in newspaper. In the upstairs bedroom, Vera swaddled the ballerina figurine in a pillowcase before stowing it in the nightstand drawer.

Her mother and grandmother provisioned a wicker hamper with food, gathered canned goods, and filled some jugs with water. They loaded the supplies and a portable gas stove into Raffi's red wagon, piling extra bedding on top. They collected their suitcases, Vera picked up Shakar's cage, the father slung the light mattresses over his shoulder, and Armen pulled the wagon. They plodded toward the garage just as the sun was going down. They were the second family to arrive and set up camp in the best corner where the floor was not slick with grease. As the evening wore on, more and more families filed in.

Armed with a flashlight, Armen and Kevo made the rounds of the garage. When they returned, Armen announced, "There are almost eighty people here. More than half our neighbors."

"Where are the rest of them?" Medz Mama asked.

Mairig answered, "In hallways or basements. In the mountains or the Bekaa Valley. The smart ones have already left Lebanon."

Vera, Taline, and Seta gathered on Vera's mattress, where they lined their dolls against a wall for a fashion show. They soon abandoned them to Raffi, who was thrilled to have the dolls to himself. Vera brushed and braided Taline's long, curly hair while beside them Seta played solitaire by flashlight.

That night the thundering and thudding above were heavy and almost continuous. The pillars of the garage shook, and small bits of cement rattled down, falling into Vera's hair and eyes. When Raffi started whimpering, Medz Mama pulled him into her lap. He wrapped the silk slip around his head, covering his face. Vera curled up next to the wall and put the pillow over her head. It sounded as though there were giants outside hurling enormous boulders at each other. The ground heaved and more grit showered down.

The fighting went on and on. It was hard to keep track of the days except for the shaft of sunlight that crept into the mouth of the garage in the morning and dimmed in the evening. Their grandmother had brought the alarm clock that usually sat on the night table in their bedroom, but to Vera time seemed strange and warped. It stretched and shrank like sticky taffy, and the hands of the clock bore little relation to the way the hours crawled by. Vera stopped putting the cover over Shakar's cage. The canary slept most of the time and didn't sing a note. It stared balefully at Vera as she tried to tempt it to eat small pieces of apple.

The water in the utility sink worked only sporadically. When it was flowing people lined up to fill their jugs. This water was for drinking and cooking. There wasn't enough to even think about washing, except for wiping dishes with a damp cloth and faces and hands with handkerchiefs. When the flashlight batteries were spent, they lit the candles.

After the first day the slop pails below were overflowing, and the stench was terrible. If the second level was purgatory, Vera imagined that the deepest level, where no one ever went, was a kind of hell where the rats had grown as big as dogs and fought over the scraps that the Devil tossed to them. Outside was also a hell where heavily armed men and boys were killing and dying. She imagined their bloodied corpses lying strewn across the streets.

The Serinossians finished the food they had brought with them, and then they had a share of the perishables donated by local shop owners. A barbecue place around the corner from the garage offered chickens that would have gone bad otherwise. The mother used their portable gas stove to boil the chickens, as did other families, and they shared them with people who had no stoves.

One afternoon when there was a pause in the shelling, Armen convinced Baba, over their mother's objections, to let him go to the house to forage in their pantry.

"It's safer for me to go than Babig. And I swear I will turn into a hen if I eat any more of that chicken," Armen said.

"If you turn into a hen, maybe you could lay some eggs," Raffi said. "I would love a hard-boiled egg."

Armen, Kevo, and Taline's brothers headed out with the red wagon. Each minute they were gone was like an hour.

"If anything happens to them," Mairig said to Baba, "I will never forgive you. In fact, I will divorce you."

Medz Mama turned her palms up and prayed out loud. "Dear God, please keep them from harm. Bring Armen and Kevork back to us, our beloved boys."

Raffi said, "I thought I was your beloved boy."

She opened her eyes and placed her hand on Raffi's head. "I have three sons and three grandsons, which makes six beloved boys. You are my smallest one."

When the boys finally arrived back, pulling behind them the wagon stacked high with canned goods, they were welcomed as heroes. Armen brought canned beans, chickpeas, lentils, and peach halves in syrup. He had scrounged up candles, batteries, and toilet paper. Vera didn't think peaches ever tasted as sweet as they did that evening when they passed the can and a fork around by candlelight.

After eight days and nights the shelling stopped, and a messenger from the *agoump* brought word that they could return to their homes. When she emerged from the garage, it took a while for Vera's eyes to adjust to the harsh sunlight. The family walked slowly back to their house through streets strewn with rubble. The Gertmenian School had been hit; all its windows were shattered, half of one wall was collapsed, and another was blackened by fire. Several nearby homes had craters in their roofs, and the house across the street had lost most of its front wall so you could see right into the living room and the second-floor bedrooms.

The family stood before their house, surveying the damage. The shutters had come off their hinges, and Vera thought that all the windows looked like empty eye sockets. But the walls and the roof were intact, which was more than could be said for some of their neighbors' houses.

Their father, picking his way through the broken glass and debris, went in the front door. The rest of them followed, stepping over the shards of glass that lay scattered on the floor like transparent knives. Pictures had fallen from the walls, and the chairs were lying on their backs and sides as though a wild man had tossed them this way and that. Windowsills, floorboards, furniture, and carpets were covered with a thick white layer of pulverized plaster and dust.

Medz Mama was pale. She leaned wearily against the wall. As the father pulled the sheet off her armchair, bits of glass clinked to the floor. He guided her by the elbow, and she sank into the chair.

Mairig sighed. "I'll get the broom."

Vera ran upstairs to her bedroom. The bureau was on its side with clothing spilling out of wrecked drawers. Splinters of glass were sprayed across the beds and the floor. Vera righted the nightstand, which had toppled forward, and pulled open its drawer. She unfolded the pillowcase to find Nora's ballerina in a dozen pieces.

Vera and Raffi drew pictures on the sidewalk with colored chalk while Armen and Kevo kicked a ball back and forth in the street.

"Will you draw a castle?" Raffi asked.

"I will," Vera said.

"And a dragon? And a princess?"

"Sure. What are you going to draw?"

"A tree and some flowers. And a rainbow over the castle."

A magic kingdom sprouted across the sidewalk. Raffi had bright chalk dust all over his pants. Vera wanted to go find Seta and Taline, but she had promised her mother she would keep Raffi entertained.

Armen and Kevo sat down on the curb near them. They were drinking sodas they had bought at the corner market.

Armen said to Kevo, "Let's ride our bikes to Bourj Hammoud."

Kevo nodded. "Let's go."

"You need permission," Vera said.

"No one asked your opinion," Armen said.

Vera grimaced at him. "You know for a fact that she would tell you no."

Armen said, "There hasn't been any fighting for almost a month. I'll go talk with Baba. Take care of the baby and leave us alone."

Raffi shouted, "I hate you."

He ran at Armen and tried to hit him, but Armen gripped Raffi's wrists.

"Stop it, Armen," Vera said.

"When I'm bigger, I'm going to beat you!" Raffi said. He tried to kick Armen in the shin, but Armen jumped his legs to one side while still grasping Raffi's wrists.

"Stop it, both of you," Vera said. "Raffi, don't pay attention to him. He's a stupid bully. Let's finish our drawing."

Armen and Kevo fetched their bicycles, and Vera and Raffi watched as the boys pedaled out of the neighborhood.

Raffi said, "He's going to be in big trouble."

Vera said, "Let's hope."

Raffi lay down on a clear spot on the sidewalk. "Will you trace around me?"

"What color?" she asked.

"Green," he said.

Once the outline was done, they added a smiling face, a shirt, a watch, pants, and striped socks. They were filling in the shoes when they heard the harsh rattle of automatic weapons. It sounded as though it was coming from the direction of the bridge.

Their mother called out the window, "Kids, come into the house right now."

Vera and Raffi gathered up the chalk and hurried in. Like a hen counting her chicks, the mother looked at each of them and glanced over their heads to confirm that Armen was behind them.

"Where is your brother?" she asked.

"He and Kevo went to Bourj Hammoud by bicycle," Vera said.

"What? How long ago did they leave?"

"Maybe twenty minutes," Vera said.

"And you let them go?"

"He never listens to me. They told Baba where they were going."

The mother stormed out, pausing to collect Tantig Anoush from next door, and continued to the father's shop. Vera, Raffi, and their grandmother trailed behind. Their father met them on the sidewalk outside his shop, and their uncle emerged from his adjacent store.

"Where are Armen and Kevork?" Mairig asked.

Baba said, "They rode their bikes to Bourj Hammoud."

"You told them they could do that?" she asked.

Amo Vahram turned up both his hands. "I know nothing. Nobody asked me."

Babig said, "They wanted to go to see the cousins. There hasn't been trouble around here for weeks."

Their mother said, "You do hear the gunfire now, don't you?"

She turned on her heel and marched back to the house. The rest of them followed. When Mairig lifted the telephone receiver, by pure luck the line was live, and she dialed her parents in Bourj Hammoud.

"Are Armen and Kevo there?" she asked. She paused for the answer. "They never made it."

Vera could hear her maternal grandmother's indistinct shouts through the receiver.

Mairig said, "Listen, please stop yelling. You need to stop and listen to me. We will make some other calls while the phone line is working. If the boys show up, call me, and if not, I'll let you know when we find them."

Baba phoned a friend who had a jewelry shop in Nor Marash just on the other side of the bridge. The jeweler was holed up in his store with customers and passersby who had been caught by the fighting. He said he could see from his shop window that several people had been shot on the bridge.

The whole family went up to the roof where they could make out two crumpled bodies on the bridge.

"I can't see that far. Are those our boys?" Medz Mama asked. "Tell me the truth."

Amo Vahram said, "It's too far for anyone to tell who they are. But I don't see any bicycles."

"I'll run down there," Baba said.

Amo Vahram said, "I'll go with you."

Tantig Anoush said, "No, I don't want you to go. Wait until the shooting is finished."

The mother said to the father, "Diran, go to the highway, but don't cross the bridge. There are snipers up the hill and on the other side, plus the rest of those fools running around with weapons."

Baba charged down the stairs, and from the roof the rest of the family watched him trot down the avenue toward the highway. When he returned, he reported that the bodies were not those of Armen and Kevork.

Raffi asked, "Are they going to be shot dead like Melkon?"

"No, little one," said Medz Mairig, "God is watching over them."

Baba said, "They're smart boys. I'm sure they found a safe place to wait until the fighting stops."

While the gunfire continued, the family gathered around the table glumly picking at the food on their plates. After dinner Mairig and Tantig Anoush washed the dishes, and the sky darkened. They sat in the living room listening to the radio, which had no reports about the fighting that they could plainly hear going on outside. After a while the night grew quiet, and it seemed that there was at least a pause in the shooting. As the father and uncle were getting ready to go out and look for the boys, Armen and Kevork walked in the front door.

Tantig Anoush and Medz Mama burst into tears.

"Where were you?" Baba asked.

"What happened?" Amo Vahram asked at the same time.

Armen said, "We made it across the river, but we didn't have time to get to the Joudigians' before the shooting started. We jumped off our bikes and pulled them into the entrance of an apartment building."

Kevork added, "We were stuck in there with a bunch of people who were shopping when the fighting broke out."

Armen said, "We thought it was the Syrians and the Lebanese Forces, but one of the guys who was with us in the building said the Kataeb had started a fight with the Dashnaks. If we back down, the Kataeb will rule the Armenians."

"After a while we started to get hungry," Kevork said.

"The shoppers had a lot of food and they shared it," Armen said. "Kevo and I ate a whole box of chocolate cookies."

Mairig said, "I'm going to slash the tires of your bicycle and lock you in your bedroom for a month."

Raffi said, "That's my bedroom too. Will I have to stay there with him, or can I sleep in your room?"

She flicked her palm at him. "Enough from you."

Medz Mama asked, "Are you boys hungry? There's food for you in the kitchen."

"After all those cookies, I'm sure they're not hungry," Mairig said.

"I'm hungry," said Armen.

"Me too," said Kevork.

"I'll make plates for you," their grandmother said, her slippers scuffing the floor as she went to the kitchen.

After they ate, Kevo went home with his parents, and Vera, Armen, and Raffi got ready for bed.

While Vera and Armen were at the bathroom sink brushing their teeth, she asked him, "Were you scared?"

Armen said, "Don't tell them, but while we were on the bridge, a bullet whizzed by my ear. An inch closer and it would have hit me. I would have been dead for sure."

She looked at him in the mirror and their eyes locked.

Vera said, "If you died, our lives would be ruined. Please think about us before you do something like that again."

Armen said, "I heard about a boy whose mother wouldn't let him out of the house. She kept him inside all the time—she didn't even let him go to school because she couldn't stand the idea that he might be kidnapped or shot by a sniper. And you know what happened to him? One night, a shell slammed through the wall of their house. He was killed in his own bed."

Vera and her grandmother lay side by side in the narrow beds in their dark room. After a few minutes it seemed that the grandmother had fallen asleep, and Vera lay listening to her parents argue in the next room. At first their voices were muffled, and Vera couldn't make out the words. But then her mother's voice rose.

"I can't take any more of this. We need to get out of this madhouse," her mother shouted. "We are surrounded by savages."

Her father's reply was a low murmur.

"Armen could have been killed today. We could all be murdered at any moment. Do you want to see one of your children laid out in a coffin? Is that what you're waiting for?" the mother exclaimed.

There was grumbling from Baba.

"I don't care about any of that," Mairig said. "And as for her, she can stay here, or she can come with us. That's her choice. If she wants to be a martyr, there's nothing to be done about it."

Their father shouted, "Have you no compassion? Is your heart made of stone?"

After this their mother lowered her voice, and Vera caught only indistinct murmurs. Soon the night was quiet, except for the ticking of the clock on the nightstand.

Vera sighed, and the grandmother said, "*Akh, yavrum*, don't worry about it."

Vera felt terrible that her grandmother had heard her mother talk like that. She was ashamed of her mother, who had sounded like a cruel witch.

"I'm sorry," Vera said.

"There's no reason to apologize. It's not your fault, child," her grandmother said.

"If they decide to go, won't you come with us?" Vera asked.

"When the Turks drove us out of Hadjin, they robbed us of our house, our garden, our orchard, and our lives. I lost my whole family, everything. Now we are to be uprooted again and tossed to the wind? I'm too old. No one will move me from this house, except to carry me to the cemetery."

She had never heard her grandmother talk about Hadjin in this way, about all that was lost. This was not like the stories she told about Sosi that made Hadjin sound like a faraway enchanted kingdom.

Vera listened to the clock. She wondered how many minutes had gone by. All Beirut was sleeping. Even the men at the checkpoints had fallen asleep with their arms wrapped around their long guns. Only she and her grandmother were lying awake in this lightless city.

"Go to sleep, my girl," Medz Mama said. "There's not much left of the night, and the sun will rise whether the rooster crows or not."

The clock ticked, the minutes marching by on small feet. Soon Vera heard her grandmother's deep, slow breathing. She could hear her own heart pumping and the blood pulsing through her veins. It sounded like waves rising and retreating along the shore.

The fighting spilled across the river into their neighborhood, with snipers on both sides of the bridge. But Vera was relieved that at least for the moment they were only shooting at each other and not firing missiles. School was closed, of course, but they could remain in their house. Vera had recurring nightmares about the garage. The rats were the size of large dogs, and when they stampeded out of the shelter, they moved in a large, churning mass toward the Bourj Hammoud garbage mountain.

Vera developed a knot of pain in her right jaw from the strain of being trapped in the house with her family. The boys' bickering was annoying, but the new way that her mother and grandmother needled each other with invisible hatpins was intolerable. Maybe it wasn't new at all. Maybe it had been going on for years, and she had never noticed it before.

Her mother lifted the phone receiver a dozen or more times in a day, slamming it down with disappointment. She was worried about her family in Bourj Hammoud. The Kataeb, who had raised their extortion fees, were dynamiting Armenian shops if their owners refused to pay. Sometimes they blew them up whether they were paid or not. The Phalangists had not yet targeted the Joudigian family market for this treatment, but when she was unable to get through to her mother, Mairig grew frantic.

The more distracted their mother was, the more Raffi tried to get her attention.

"Mama, Mama," he said. "What should I do now? Will you play with me? Can I have something to eat?"

"Stop pestering me," she told him. "Go ask your grandmother."

She had even less patience with Armen, who was either picking fights or sneaking up to the roof, which their mother said would end in his being shot in the head by a sniper.

"Where is your brother?" she asked Vera.

"I don't know. Maybe in his bedroom."

"Go look," she commanded.

Vera didn't find him on the second floor, so she climbed the stairs to the roof. She stuck her head out the door. There was Armen leaning against the wall holding a cigarette between his thumb and finger.

She asked him, "When did you start smoking?"

"A while ago," he said.

"And where do you get the cigarettes?"

"I do errands for the comrades, and they give them to me." He put the cigarette to his lips and inhaled. Then he pointed toward a building near the bridge. "There's a Lebanese Forces sniper on the top floor. The comrades are stationed at the Massis Club and Nigol Touman in Bourj Hammoud."

"Can I try your cigarette?" she asked.

"No sister of mine is ever going to touch a cigarette."

He was skinny and shorter than she by almost a head, so his bravado sounded ridiculous. She told him, "You need to put that thing out. She sent me to find you."

Their mother shouted up the stairs, "Armen and Vera, get down here now. If I come up there, you will be very sorry."

Armen stubbed out the cigarette in the hibiscus pot. He grabbed a sprig of mint from another pot and chewed on a leaf. He rubbed the other leaves on his fingers.

The next afternoon, Vera, her brothers, and Kevo were at the kitchen table drawing while their grandmother mended socks. Medz Mama slid the wooden darning egg into the toe, her needle flashing in and out as she wove thread to fill the hole.

Their mother picked up the phone for the hundredth time, and at that moment there was a dial tone. She quickly composed the number, and when the call connected, she said, "Finally, we reached you."

They all jumped up from the table and gathered around as Mairig talked. Vera could hear only one half of the conversation, but her mother repeated what she was being told in disbelief.

"Twenty Armenians killed? No doctor? The dental surgeon is treating the wounded. How many hostages? Anyone we know? Ah. Not him."

The line abruptly went dead, and their mother slammed down the receiver.

"What are we doing here?" she yelled. "Why are we in this doomed city? This country is cursed."

"Don't be upset, Mama," Raffi said.

Their mother turned to her mother-in-law and said, "I blame you. You are the one keeping us here. He won't leave you and you won't go. Do you want us all to be murdered? Are the dead calling your name? Should we join our ancestors massacred by the Turks? I won't let it happen. I won't."

Medz Mama said, "I told you to go. This is my home and I'm staying here, but you, you are free to go whenever, wherever you want. I'm not holding you."

Raffi said, "I don't want to go. I don't want to leave Medz Mama."

Armen shouted, "What's the matter with all of you? I'm not leaving Beirut. We can't desert the comrades."

"Stop it, all of you. We're not going anywhere," Vera said.

"And who put you in charge of anything, miss?" her mother asked. "Look at Raffi's drawing and then tell me you want to stay."

Vera glanced down at the kitchen table at the picture Raffi had made. His paper was covered with small figures carrying guns. There were black dashes across the page for flying bullets. He had drawn the church with a missile crashed into its roof. In front of the church, the priest was lying on the ground with a circle of blood around him. Vera glanced at Armen's paper and saw that he had drawn the insignias of the three Armenian political parties and the flags of the Lebanese militias. Vera stared at her own drawing. It was the garden from her grandmother's stories about Hadjin. There were flowers, a rabbit, a fox, and a tree covered with mulberries.

"You see," their mother said, turning again to her mother-in-law. "My children will die here, and it's because of you."

Their grandmother said tearfully, "Please don't talk to me like that. I'm sorry. I'm an old woman. I'm not well. It's too late for me to fly like a bird to another place. But you go. I'll tell my son to take you away."

Their grandmother started swaying on her feet.

"Please sit, Medz Mama," Vera said, guiding her toward a chair.

The old woman slumped into the seat. She plucked a handkerchief from the pocket of her apron and wiped tears from her face.

Their father walked into the kitchen just then. "What's for supper?"

Their mother ran out of the room and stormed up the stairs, slamming the bedroom door.

Baba looked at the rest of them questioningly. "What's the matter with her?"

"Take her and your children away from here," Medz Mama said. "Don't stay here because of me. Vahram will be here if I need anything. Go to your brother in New Jersey. Go to California. Go to Australia. Just go."

The teacher stood at the front of the classroom with a new boy. "This is Alex. His family has moved here from Kantari, and I hope that you will make him feel welcome. Alex, why don't you say a few words about yourself."

The boy's eyebrows shot up, and he bowed his head slightly. Two girls in the second row started giggling. Vera glanced at Isabel and Rita, who were the most popular girls in the grade. They wore blue eye shadow and curled their eyelashes with a special gadget that Vera had seen on sale in the pharmacy. Isabel's face was framed by dark curls, and Rita's long black hair looked like she pressed it with an iron. They feigned friendly interest and then knocked the breath out of you with a cruel remark. Vera avoided them as much as possible. While they giggled at the new boy's discomfort, Vera imagined using her pen to shoot poisoned darts at them. Isabel and Rita lay sprawled on the classroom floor.

Finally, Alex said, "Thank you, Digin. I am happy to be here with you all. May I please sit down?"

"Of course, dear," the teacher said. "Take that empty desk by the window."

This desk, which was right in front of Vera's, had recently been vacated by a boy named Antranig who had moved to Montreal. Antranig had leered up girls' skirts on the staircase. He had picked his nose and wiped it under his chair, and he had smelled like dirty socks.

After Alex slid into the seat, Vera studied the back of his head. Unlike the boys who had adopted the shaggy hairdos of the comrades, Alex's hair was short and there was a tender strip of skin showing between the bottom of his hairline and the top of his collar.

At recess, the boys invited Alex to join their soccer game. He maneuvered the ball through a forest of legs to kick it between the orange traffic cones that served as goalposts. His teammates slapped him on the back in congratulations. Vera watched as he scored two more goals, securing his status among the boys.

When the class headed back into the building at the end of recess, Isabel and Rita ran up to Alex and appeared to be asking him a question.

Vera couldn't make out their words, but she heard their laughter.

Alex looked at them as though they were speaking an unknown language. He shook his head and walked away.

The girls glanced at each other, rolled their eyes, and laughed again.

In homeroom the next morning, Alex turned around and asked Vera if he could borrow a pen, as his had run out of ink. She opened her pencil case and offered him his choice.

"That's a lot of pens and pencils," he said, deftly twirling the pen he had selected. "I never have more than one."

"Taline's father owns a stationery shop, and she gave me this case for my birthday."

"Which one is Taline?" he asked.

"She's sitting in front of you."

"Is she your best friend?" he asked.

"She and Seta are my best friends."

"Which one is Seta?"

She pointed Seta out. "She's on the other side. Her father owns a candy shop."

"For someone whose father has a candy shop, she's very skinny. And what's the name of the girl in front of her?"

"That's Isabel."

"She has weird eyebrows," he said.

Isabel had given herself clown eyebrows like Tantig Anahid's. Vera was surprised Alex had mentioned them because she didn't think that boys noticed things like that.

The teacher rapped on her desk with a ruler. "Children, children, settle down now. I have some announcements to make."

When Alex turned to face front, Vera noticed that his ears fit neatly along the side of his head. His dark hair was smooth and glossy and looked like it would be soft to the touch.

"Every time I turn around, you're staring at the back of his head," Taline said as they were walking down the hill after school.

"What am I supposed to do? He sits right in front of me," Vera said.

Taline said, "I don't remember you looking like that when Antranig was sitting in front of you."

"Antranig was disgusting," said Seta.

"I know," said Taline. "But that's not the point. Vera likes Alex."

"Everyone likes Alex," Seta said. "Except Isabel and Rita, because he's not interested in them."

Some of the boys in their class—the ones with thick, dark hair starting to sprout above their upper lips—eyed Isabel and Rita like hungry squirrels. The rest of them displayed little interest in girls, and most of the girls in their grade had crushes on the older boys who were safely beyond their reach. Alex ignored Isabel and Rita, but he often turned around in his chair to talk to Vera. And in art class, he had asked to see the sketches in her folder.

"These are great," he said, flipping through the drawings. "I like this one the best." He held up a self-portrait that she had made with colored pencils. "It really looks like you."

"I worked on it a long time," Vera said.

"Do you think you could make a portrait of me and Aline? It would be a great birthday present for my mother."

Alex's sister Aline was in the sixth grade. He had introduced her to Vera in the chapel one day, and after that Aline waved to her in the hall.

"Sure. The easiest would be if I did it from a photo," she said.

"I'll bring you the picture tomorrow."

"When do you need it?" she asked.

"Her birthday is in three weeks."

When they were exiting the schoolyard, Alex pointed out the balcony of his second-floor apartment in a building across the street. Two women were at a table in the sun having coffee.

"There's my mother," he said. "She's wearing the green dress. The other one is our neighbor."

His mother leaned over the railing and called to Alex, "Where's your sister?"

"I don't know," he said.

Suddenly, Aline appeared on the balcony behind the mother and waved.

"Ask your friend to join us," his mother said.

"You want to come upstairs?" he asked.

Taline and Seta were watching as they waited for Vera on the corner.

"Maybe another time," she told him.

The next day in homeroom, Alex passed an envelope to Vera. Inside she found three photographs. One was a color snapshot

of Alex and Aline standing on the Corniche with the sea behind them. There was a black and white studio portrait of the
two of them, and the third was a wallet-sized school photo
of Alex.

As Vera, her mother, and brothers walked home from the market, each of them carrying cloth sacks filled with groceries, their mother again tried to paint a picture for them of the beautiful life that awaited them in New Jersey.

"Your uncle said all the houses have gardens. We can plant vegetables, flowers, and maybe even a few fruit trees. And the electricity and the water will work all the time. Imagine that."

As her mother talked, Vera walked in silence, and her brothers also said nothing.

"When we get there, I'll buy you each a special gift," Mairig said. "What would you like?"

"A horse," said Raffi.

Mairig laughed. "Why not a giraffe?"

"If I can't have a horse, can I have a dog?" Raffi said.

"We could certainly manage a kitten. What do you want, Vera?" she asked.

Vera had no interest in anything they might find in America, but she didn't want to enrage her mother. She said, "I don't know."

"Well, think about it. And what about you, Armen?" their mother said.

Armen replied, "I'm not leaving here unless it's in a coffin."

Their mother dropped the grocery bags she was carrying, reached out, and lunged at his ear. He ducked away, dashing ahead, the bags swinging against his legs as he ran.

Now that Armen and Kevo were students at the Central

High School, they often went in the afternoon with other boys to the Hunchak *agoump* in Khalil Badawi. Their comrades had taught them how to disassemble and reassemble the firearms. One afternoon on their way down the hill from school, Vera heard her brother and Kevo describing the guns to Taline's brothers.

Armen said, "The AK-47—the 'klashin'—is by far the best weapon. But we also work with the shotguns and the sniper rifles."

"Did they teach you how to shoot?" Sako asked.

"The Kataeb militia controls this part of the city, so you need to go to Anjar for weapons training. Maybe next year they'll take us. Last week some guys in the Dashnak club asked me to carry a message to Phalangist headquarters. When I went inside, I saw some of their gear. They even had a rocket launcher."

Here Armen paused to open his school satchel, pulling out his notebook, which was filled with drawings of the weapons. The boys gathered around to study the drawings. When Vera, Taline, and Seta leaned in, Armen slapped the notebook shut, glaring at them.

"Do you know what your pumpkin head of a brother has been up to?" her mother asked Vera.

"What do you mean?" Vera asked, stalling for time. She wondered which of her brother's antics her mother had heard about.

"At the *shirkets* this morning, one of the ladies told me that Armen has been carrying messages between the clubs. It made me wonder what other mischief he might be up to. He does seem to spend a lot of time up on the roof."

Mairig then marched up the stairs to the second floor and

from there she continued up to the roof. Vera and Raffi stood at the bottom of the stairs listening.

"What if she finds his bullet collection?" Raffi whispered.

Their mother shouted, "Vera, Raffi, come up here now."

"I'm scared," Raffi said.

Vera took his hand, and the two of them climbed the stairs. They emerged on the roof as their mother, who was rummaging through a cardboard box, pulled out a handgun. It was so old and rusty Vera couldn't imagine it still worked.

"Help me with this," their mother said, pointing at the carton.

As they dragged the box down the stairs, Mairig spewed insults against the comrades, the Kataeb, and all the men of Beirut. In the front hall, she pulled the pistol out of the box and held it up to show it to their grandmother.

"Look what I found. Armen was hiding this behind your plants."

Medz Mama put her hands to her face. "*Vahkh, vahkh,* get rid of that thing before someone gets hurt. Throw it into the ash barrel."

"That's Armen's bullet collection," Raffi said. "All the boys have them."

Their mother said, "And what about the gun? Is this part of his gun collection?"

Raffi chewed his lip, shifting from one foot to the other. "I think he has only one gun."

Their mother said, "Vera, help me bring this to your father's shop."

"It's too heavy," she replied.

Their mother barked, "Take one side."

By the time they arrived at the shop, they were sweating, and her mother's fury was overflowing its banks.

She barked at the father, "Look at what your son has hidden behind your mother's flowerpots."

Baba said, "All the boys collect this stuff."

She extracted the pistol from the box. "Who gave this to him? The comrades? What are they doing giving children guns?"

"He's started to have a moustache," he said.

"Diran, what kind of lunatic thing is that to say?" she yelled.

"Calm down, Araxi," he said. "I'll talk to him."

She shouted, "That's not good enough. Stop dragging your feet. I want you to go to the American Embassy to apply for the visa."

He said, "Okay. Okay, I'll go."

"When?" she demanded.

"Tomorrow," he said.

Vera's shoulders started heaving up and down, and a strange gasping sound escaped from her mouth. Her parents turned to look at her as though they had suddenly remembered that she was standing there.

Her mother said, "What am I going to do with this one? She is weeping again. I blame the war for that too. What's the matter with you now?"

Vera didn't want her father to apply for a visa. She didn't want to abandon their house, their neighborhood, her grandmother, her friends, her school, and Shakar the canary.

Vera said, "You can throw away the gun, but please don't take away Armen's bullet collection. All the boys have them, but his is the very best."

"My Lord, if one more person tells me that all the boys have them, I'm going to shoot someone." She pointed the gun's muzzle at the ceiling.

Baba said, "Give that to me. I'm going to take it to the

agoump and have a talk with the guys. And leave me to deal with Armen."

"Can't we send Raffi to get it? He's old enough. I'll write it on a piece of paper for him to show the pharmacist," Vera said.

Raffi asked, "Send me to get what?"

"Nothing," their mother said. "Vera is going now. You do your homework."

Vera walked up the avenue. She was dreading the moment when she would put the pale blue cardboard box of menstrual pads on the counter in front of the pharmacist. All her friends, her mother, her aunts, and their friends also needed these things. Why then did she find it so embarrassing? It had something to do with the way her grandmother said, "Don't let anyone see your bottom. Make sure they can't see your panties. Cover your shame."

"Hello, Vera," Baron Ouzonian, the pharmacist, said. "How is your grandmother? No one at home is sick, I hope?"

"We're all fine, thank you. I'm here to pick up a few things for my mother," she told him.

She placed a tube of toothpaste, a packet of hair clips, and the blue box on the counter in front of him.

"Do you have chewing gum?" she asked.

"Right there," he said, pointing to her left on the counter.

She handed him the gum. When she fumbled in her purse for money, a coin dropped onto the white tiled floor.

As she bent down to retrieve it, the pharmacist said, "Ah Vera, you're all grown up now. I remember when your head didn't even reach the counter."

He didn't believe her ruse. He knew that she had not bought the pads for her mother. He knew she was the shameful one. Her face was crimson as she took the bag from him. "Thank you so much, Baron."

The bell jangled as she exited. On the sidewalk, she exhaled deeply. The ordeal was over. At least no one else had been in the store to witness her humiliation.

"Vera," someone called.

She looked up. One of the guys in green khakis at the checkpoint was waving to her.

Michel strode toward her. The other guys at the checkpoint were busy inspecting a car they had stopped.

"What are you doing here?" she asked.

"New assignment," he said, stepping closer to her. "You live around here?"

"Not far," she said.

He was so close that she could smell his sweat. She thought of offering him a piece of chewing gum, but then she remembered what else was in her bag.

"I'm late," she said, rushing past him.

"See you soon," he called after her.

The next afternoon as Vera, Taline, and Seta walked home from school, Michel hailed them as they approached the checkpoint.

"Girls, girls, I want to talk with you." He smiled at them.

"That's him," Vera said.

"He's so handsome. He looks just like Bachir Gemayel," said Taline.

Seta said, "You and your Bachir. Let's ignore this guy."

He walked closer. "Hello, girls, I'm Michel, and I'm a friend of Vera's. What are your names?"

"I'm Taline, and she's Seta," Taline said.

"Nice to meet you. Do you think you can talk Vera into having a coffee with me sometime?"

Seta said, "Her mother would ground her for even looking at you. Please move out of our way."

Michel laughed as the girls hurried by.

"Bye, girls. See you next time, Vera!" he said.

As they turned the corner, Taline said, "There was no reason for you to be so rude."

Seta ignored her. "We should take the long way around to avoid that guy. He's a dolt."

Taline said, "That's silly. He's just being friendly. He's so good-looking. And I love that little white scarf. It's so chic."

The next day, Vera stayed after school to work on the gift for Alex's mother. The art teacher gave her a sheet of fine drawing paper and a tin case of graphite pencils. As the teacher was leaving, she said, "When you are finished, dear girl, please shut the lights. Vahan will lock the door after he cleans."

Vera studied the black and white studio portrait of Alex and his sister. She sat at the table and laid out a grid of faint pencil lines on the paper, then carefully transposed the two figures. When the janitor arrived with his mop and bucket, she looked up at the clock and realized she had been working for over two hours.

"Time to go home, young lady," the janitor said.

"Sorry, Baron Vahan. Thank you. Have a good night." She slid the drawing into her folder, ran out of the school and down the steps.

As she approached the checkpoint, her pulse quickened. She was afraid she would see Michel and she was also afraid that she would not see him. And there he was, the white scarf, the birthmark on his cheek, and the hawk-like eyes.

"You're late," he said. "The other girls passed by a while ago."

"I stayed after school," she said.

He asked, "Were you in trouble?"

"I was working on a drawing," she said.

"So, you're an artist," he said.

"I don't know about that. But I like to draw," she said.

"Do you like me too?" he asked.

She was taken off guard by the question and felt her cheeks flush. "Maybe." She rushed past him and heard his laughter behind her.

When he saw the finished drawing, Alex said, "I love it. Now you need to sign it."

"Why?" Vera asked.

"When you are a famous artist, my mother will say, Vera Serinossian made this for me when she was a girl."

She did as he asked. Then she held out the envelope with the three photos. "Don't forget these."

"Oh, you were meant to keep this one." He pulled out the pocket-sized school portrait and handed it to her. "You didn't see what I wrote on the back?"

She turned the photo over and saw the words, "For my friend Vera."

Several days later, Vera followed Alex and Aline out of the schoolyard, across the street, and into the lobby of their building. Their mother opened the apartment door as soon as they stepped onto the landing.

"Come in, come in. I'm so happy you are here, Vera. Alex says such nice things about you. And that portrait you drew was my favorite gift."

"I'm so glad you liked it, Digin Seferian," Vera said.

"Please call me Anita Tantig," she said.

Their apartment reminded Vera of Nora's place, although there were not so many mirrors and gold knickknacks. Vera's framed drawing was in a place of honor on the wall in the dining room. There was a glass bowl full of crystal fruit sitting in the middle of a polished wood table. In the kitchen, Tantig

Anita had arranged tea and juice and cookies on a copper tray. She carried the tray to the balcony, and they sat around a mosaic tile tabletop.

"Alex tells me you live in Hadjin. Do you know Sako Hadjinian, the watchmaker?" Tantig Anita asked.

"He and my father play backgammon together," Vera said.

"He's married to my second cousin, Ani. Our family is from Marash. Aline, you've had enough cookies. Alex, go get your oud and play something for us. Did you know, Vera, that Alex has been studying oud since he was six? It's sad that his teacher is on the other side of the Green Line."

Alex returned with his oud. Reminding Vera of a ripe fig that had been cut in half, the instrument was beautiful, with three intricate rosettes set into its blond wood face. He played, his fingers moving with the same quickness and grace he showed on the soccer field.

His mother insisted that Alex walk Vera home. On the way down the hill, the sky was a clear, cloudless blue. Vera could smell the flowering jasmine, there were magenta bougainvillea vines climbing up a wall that they passed, and a cascading jacaranda was visible above a walled garden. Alex was telling her about the special oud, made with four kinds of wood, that he was saving money to buy.

When Hadjin was within sight, they paused on the avenue. People and cars streamed past. It was awkward standing there, but she was reluctant to say goodbye.

Alex said, "Well, here you are. I'll see you tomorrow."

And with that he turned back up the hill.

Ahead of her she saw piles of litter around the sandbagged checkpoint. The militiamen stared at her bare legs in a way that made her wish her skirt were longer and the socks taller. She didn't see Michel.

Suddenly, he emerged from the corner shop holding a packet of cigarettes. He unwrapped the cellophane from the pack, tore off the top, and extracted a cigarette.

"Vera!" Michel called. He walked toward her. "You want one?"

"No thank you," she said.

"You came by just at the right time. I have a break now, and there's something I want to show you," he said.

"What is it?"

"We have an apartment near here that's full of art."

"What kind of art?"

"Paintings and drawings," he said.

"Whose apartment is it?" she asked.

"Some rich people who left for Paris. It's been requisitioned."

Now that the militia had claimed the apartment as their own, she wondered if they would make off with the art and the rugs. Apartments like these, empty of their owners, were soon empty of their furnishings.

"What kind of paintings and drawings?" she pressed.

"I'm not the artist. You tell me," he said with a smile.

They walked up the avenue a few blocks toward Mar Mikhael, and then turned onto a side street. They entered a broad lobby with marble floors and Michel led the way up the stairs. When they reached the wide landing, he turned and seized her by the shoulders, pushing her against the wall. She gasped in surprise, and he pressed his mouth to hers, forcing his tongue into her mouth. As the thick, wet muscle thrashed against her tongue and teeth, she knew she had made a terrible mistake. When his hand clamped her left breast, she twisted out of his grasp.

As she moved toward the steps, he seized her arm. His fingers dug into her flesh, all the way down to the bone.

"You're hurting me," she said. "Please let go."

"Don't play games with me. Why did you come here?" he said.

"I wanted to see the art," she said.

He snorted with laughter without releasing his grip on her arm.

"I have to go," she said. "I have a boyfriend."

The words had emerged instinctively. She had wagered that, rather than enraging him more, marking herself as someone else's property would prompt him to let go. For three long seconds she watched a series of emotions play over his face.

His hold on her slackened, and he gave her a little shove. "You should have told me. I wouldn't have wasted my time."

She escaped down the stairs, racing out of the building. Her arm throbbed, and her breathing was fast and shallow. She was ashamed that she was so stupid as to believe he had wanted to show her some paintings. She could imagine what her mother would say. Only bad girls follow a boy like that, and you know how they end up: half naked and dead in a gutter.

Vera didn't want to go home until the pain in her arm had subsided. Navigating the back streets, she headed toward the candy store, hoping to find Seta. Vera peered in the window, relieved that her friend was sitting alone behind the counter.

Seta's eyes widened when she saw Vera's face. "What happened to you?"

"You promise you won't tell anyone?" Vera asked.

"Of course," Seta said.

"Not even Taline?"

"That blabbermouth?"

"Michel grabbed me," Vera said. She was too mortified to say the rest of what he did.

"Did he hurt you?"

Vera pushed up her sleeve. On her upper arm his fingers had left marks that looked like purple plums.

Seta said, "You're lucky he didn't do something worse."

Vera flinched, thinking of what might have happened, but she said, "You sound like my mother."

"Just because she's your mother doesn't mean she's always wrong," Seta said.

Vera, Seta, and Taline were watching the boys play soccer in the schoolyard. Alex, who had the ball, ricocheted through a thicket of boys to score another goal.

"He's so fast," Taline said.

Seta said, "Too bad there aren't matches with other schools. With him as the captain, we would win the tournament."

"Maybe next year," Taline said. "I mean, how long can this stupid war go on?"

Seta said, "My father thinks it's going to get bad again. He says he can feel it. The Phalangists are preparing for something."

"Why does your father tell you depressing things like that? What good does it do anybody?" Taline said.

"You'd rather not know?" Seta said.

"Oh, forget about it. Let's go," said Taline. "I'm sick of this game. My father wants my help in the shop this afternoon. Of course, he never asks the twins to do anything."

Seta said, "They're probably with Armen and Kevo on the train bridge setting off firecrackers or torturing a cat."

"Are you coming with us?" Taline asked Vera.

"I'm going to stay," she answered.

Taline said, "She's waiting for her boyfriend."

"He's my friend," Vera said.

"It's impossible for a girl and a boy to be friends," Taline said.

Seta said, "Of course you would say something like that."

When the game was finished, Alex dribbled the ball over to

the bench where she was sitting. His face was ruddy and glistening with sweat.

"My mother told me she was going to bake a cake for you," he said. "She's happy you're going to do a drawing of her boy with his oud."

"I'm glad she likes me."

"Are you kidding? She loves you," Alex said.

At the apartment, Tantig Anita had the brass tray waiting for them. Alex and Vera went to the balcony where the late afternoon sun cast gold light over the potted plants and the flowering vines that grew along the railing.

When Vera reached for the water pitcher, her blouse sleeve hiked up.

Alex said, "What's that on your arm?"

She had forgotten about the bruises. They were still purple in the center, but the edges were a sickly yellow. She pulled her sleeve over them.

"I tripped and bumped into something," she said. Her mother and grandmother had believed this.

"That's not what it looks like to me," he said. "What happened?"

"There is a guy at the checkpoint who stopped me a couple of times when I walked by after school. The other day he grabbed me, and I had to run away."

"He must have grabbed you hard to leave marks like that. Is he still bothering you?"

"I lied and said I have a boyfriend, so I think he'll leave me alone."

"What's his name?" Alex asked.

"It's not important," she said. "Let's go inside so I can start the drawing."

When it was time for Vera to leave, Alex offered to walk

her home. On their way to Hadjin, without discussing it, they took back streets, avoiding the checkpoint.

At her corner, Alex said, "If that guy comes near you again, I want you to promise that you will tell me."

She said, "I don't think there's much you can do about it. He has a gun."

He said, "My father is on the party's central committee. They have contacts with Kataeb leadership. They would take care of him."

After school Vera went to her father's shop. He was teaching her how to help him with his account books. Through the front window she could see him leaning over the lathe.

He switched off the machine when she came through the door.

"Hello, *anoushig*," he said. "How was school?"

"It was fine."

"Nothing to report?"

"Not really."

"Do you have a lot of homework tonight?" her father asked.

"We have an English test tomorrow."

"It's good that you have been studying English. We will need your help as an interpreter when we get to New Jersey."

Nobody had mentioned New Jersey in weeks and weeks, and after she had helped her father fill out the visa application, Vera had hoped that the whole idea of America had been forgotten.

"The visa came through?" Vera said.

He nodded. "Yesterday."

"Have you told her?"

"This morning," he said.

"We're going?"

"Yes," he said.

"When do we leave?"

"When school gets out."

Her stomach lurched. She couldn't believe it was so soon.

"What are you going to do about all this?" she said, gesturing at the racks of tools and the stacks of wood. On one shelf there was an array of small woodcarvings he had made over the years—animals, a bicycle, and a miniature of the church. She looked down at the scarred linoleum littered with thin curling corkscrews of wood, and at the bits of sawdust on the tops and in the welts of his worn brown shoes.

He said, "The hand tools I will ship to New Jersey. Your Uncle Mardig convinced his boss to hire me to work on those fancy houses they're building. I'll lay parquet floors and make built-in bookcases. Vahram will watch the shop here. Maybe when the war ends, we can come back."

Later, when Armen and Vera were alone in the kitchen doing their homework at the table, he suddenly threw his pencil across the room, and it bounced off the wall.

He said, "I'm not going."

"Yes, you are," Vera said.

"She might change her mind," he said.

"No, she won't."

"I'll stay here with Medz Mama and Kevo."

"They won't let you."

"Our parents are cowards and traitors."

"Think about all the other families who have already left."

"They are all cowards and traitors. They have no loyalty, no national feeling, and no honor," he said.

"Let's not say anything at school. I don't want the teachers looking at me like I'm about to die of a horrible disease."

"Being a traitor is a horrible disease," Armen said. "You don't want to go to New Jersey, do you?"

"No, I don't," she said. "But what choice do we have?"

"You could do what Nora did, get pregnant and marry Alex," he said.

"Thanks for the great suggestion," Vera said. "How did you know about Nora?"

"Her dolt of a brother told half the school."

Vera and Alex planned to go to his apartment that afternoon so she could finish the oud drawing. She thought it was one of the best things she had done and was looking forward to showing it to him when it was finished. She hadn't yet told anyone—not even Seta and Taline—about the visa.

As they exited the school gate, Alex said, "My mother had to take Aline to the dentist. She has a toothache."

In other words, they would have the apartment to themselves.

In the salon, Alex took his place on the gold velvet couch. He picked up the oud and started playing.

"What's that song?" she asked as she sketched.

"My own composition," he said.

"It's very nice," she said.

He played on and she continued drawing. The minutes slid by like silk.

After a while she said, "Would you do me a favor and stop playing for a few minutes? Just hold your hands in position for a chord."

He stilled his fingers on the strings.

"And please look down the way you were before."

He dropped his eyes.

"Perfect," she said. Now the only sounds in the room were the scratch of her pencil on the paper and the ticking of the wall clock.

When she was done, she moved to the couch to show him the portrait. They sat side by side, the velvet upholstery smooth against the back of Vera's legs. She felt a pulse in the air between her shoulder and Alex's. The space between them was filled with one thought: should she tell him about the visa? She knew that telling him would make that space permanent. She wavered.

"Alex," she started.

Just then he placed his arm along the back of the couch behind her and stared intently at the drawing.

"It's great," he said, sliding his arm around her shoulder.

She started to laugh.

He pulled back. "What's funny?"

"I'm nervous," she said. "It's the first time we've been alone like this." And, she thought without saying it, maybe the last.

He placed his fingers on her cheek, leaning toward her until their foreheads were touching. Suddenly, she remembered Michel and his awful tongue. She pushed the thought away. That had not counted. This would be her first kiss. Their noses bumped, and it was a little awkward at first, but then somehow perfect.

Vera and Alex leaned back against the couch, and she rested her head on his shoulder. She wanted to stay exactly like this for a long time, her face against the smooth cotton of his shirt, breathing in his scent, feeling the rise and fall of his chest.

He asked, "Have you seen that guy at the checkpoint again?"

Vera was surprised by the question. "No. I have been avoiding the checkpoint. Why do you ask?"

"Well, now you really have a boyfriend," he said.

She smiled.

He said, "You know, I've never been to your house. I haven't met your family, except for Armen. Aren't you going to invite me over?'

She knew this was when she should tell him about the visa

and about the fact that she and her family were leaving Beirut. But she was a coward, and she couldn't do it. She kissed him instead.

A few days later Alex was waiting for Vera in the school courtyard after the last class bell rang.

He said, "Why didn't you tell me?"

She asked, "Who told you?"

"Does it matter?" he said. "Everyone knew except for me."

"Only the people in our neighborhood knew. We asked our friends not to say anything at school. I'm sorry you didn't hear it from me first."

He was quiet, and she couldn't read his face, which was set like a mask.

Vera said, "When the visa came through, I thought I should tell you, but I didn't want to spoil everything."

"Well, you pretty much did that," he said.

And with that, he walked away, leaving her stunned. She had expected him to be upset, but not angry at her. It wasn't her fault. The blame belonged to her mother, her father, the Lebanese Forces, and all the rest of them, but not to her.

She didn't look for Seta and Taline. She rushed down the steps, and like a homing pigeon, she took the regular route toward Hadjin. When she went past the checkpoint on the avenue, Michel was near the cement roadblock. She saw a flicker of recognition in his eyes and then he glanced away in disgust.

She slipped into the house and sped to her bedroom. She didn't want to talk to any of them. She closed the door quietly, and then flung herself onto the bed. She lay on her back, putting the crook of one arm over her eyes. Alex despised her. Michel also despised her, although why should she care about him? She loathed herself. The weight of it all pinned her to the bed as though the wall of the house had collapsed on top of her.

She heard a soft tapping at the door.

"Vera?" Raffi said.

He opened the door a crack. "Can I come in?"

"Yes," she told him.

He sat on the edge of her bed.

"Are you crying because we are leaving?" he asked.

"I'm crying about everything. You wouldn't understand."

"I do understand," he shouted, jumping up and running from the room.

The next day in homeroom, Alex sat rigidly facing the front of the classroom. Tiny arrows seemed to be flying at her from the back of his head. What if he never spoke to her again? It was going to be miserable to leave, but even worse if he refused to say goodbye. She had to do something. She quickly composed some words on a slip of paper.

> Dear Alex,
> I'm so sorry. Please forgive me.
> *Sirov*,
> Vera

She carefully folded the paper into a small triangle. Waiting until the teacher's back was turned, she dropped it over his shoulder onto the desktop. She half expected him to brush it to the floor. But he opened it, and she watched as he read it. He didn't turn, but she saw the tension in his shoulders slacken. He slid the paper into the back of his notebook.

As the bell rang at the end of homeroom and people started springing from their chairs, she leaned forward and said, "Can we talk later?"

He said, "Meet me by the gate at the end of the day."

"Where should we go?" she asked him.

"There's a café with a garden near the Orthodox Hospital."

She didn't have any money, and after glancing at her face, he understood.

"I'm inviting you," he told her.

This made her feel better. If you hated someone, you wouldn't offer to pay.

They didn't talk on the ten-minute walk from the school. When they were seated at a round table in the café's cloistered garden, Vera and Alex sat in silence until the waiter had set their drinks in front of them.

"Will you accept my apology?" Vera asked.

He shrugged. "What's the point? You're leaving next week."

"That's why it's important."

He said, "Sometimes once things are broken, they can't be put back together."

"You sound like my grandmother. 'Once a loaf of bread is cut in half, it can't be made whole again.'"

"Exactly," he said.

He sounded sour. She wanted to make him laugh. If he laughed, she might be able to win him over.

"My grandmother also says, 'If there were wisdom in beards, then goats would be prophets,'" she told him.

He laughed. "Okay. That's funny. I never heard that one before."

It had worked. The key had turned in the lock.

"Are you still angry?" she asked.

He said, "Yes. Because I am sad."

"Am I still your girlfriend?"

"No. Maybe. Yes. But only until you leave," he said.

She looked at him. He seemed younger, almost like a small child.

"I guess that's fair," she said.

"No, it's not fair. None of this is fair."

They filed into the chapel for the final service of the year. As usual, Taline was on one side of Vera, and Seta on the other. Vera turned around to look at Alex, who was seated in the pew behind them with the other boys in their grade.

The Badveli told them, "Dear children, we are saying goodbye today for the year, but God willing, we will be with each other again in the autumn. We should all pray that the war will end. I have faith that Our Lord will protect us, and that the security situation won't get any worse."

Vera had decided that most of what the Badveli said was wrong, so she assumed his speech that morning indicated that there would be another outbreak of violence in the coming weeks. He droned on, but she was no longer listening. She wondered if she would miss even this—the white walls and dark wood of the sanctuary, the pews filled with her classmates and the younger children, the stained-glass windows, and the minister at his pulpit showering them with Bible verses and bad advice. These friends, this school, her extended family, her neighborhood, the church, and their community were her whole world, and soon she would be torn from it the way a page is ripped from a book.

After school, she and Alex sat on the steps of his apartment building drinking cold sodas from glass bottles. Alex chewed on the top of the red and white striped straw.

"It's so hot," Vera said. "The bottles are sweating."

Alex said, "My shirt is plastered to my back."

They watched as a mother and three kids strolled by on the

sidewalk in front of them. Vera felt sadness bearing down on her again, and she leaned for support on the rough stucco wall beside her.

"I made something for you." She handed him a portrait of the two of them that was small enough to fit into the center of his palm. She had worked carefully on this miniature, capturing the exact shape of his eyes and the way he tipped his head slightly to the left when he smiled. Their shoulders were touching, and she was wearing her favorite striped shirt and had her hair pulled back into a ponytail. She had slipped the drawing into a tiny plastic sleeve she found at the stationery shop. She imagined that Alex would tuck the drawing into a drawer, and that years from now when he came across it, he would think, "Ah, she was such a lovely girl, that Vera."

He said, "Thanks. It's perfect. And you have been my best friend."

When Vera approached the house, she saw her grandmother sitting in a rattan chair on the sidewalk. Sparrows hopped at her feet pecking at breadcrumbs she had scattered.

"I've been waiting for you, *yavrum*," Medz Mama said. She stood and brushed the crumbs from her apron.

"Where is everyone?" Vera asked.

"Your mother and Raffi are still at school. Where is Armen?"

"He and Kevo went to the club," she said.

They sat at the kitchen table, and her grandmother put a plate of freshly baked cookies in front of Vera.

"I made these for you," Medz Mama said.

"I'm not hungry," Vera said.

"You are sad because you told your friends farewell," Medz Mama said.

Vera nodded.

Her grandmother inhaled and sighed. "I'm sorry, but there is more bad news. I found Shakar at the bottom of his cage. I buried him because I knew you and Raffi would not like to see him like that."

Vera dropped her face into her hands. In her head, she heard her mother's voice saying, "People are being kidnapped and murdered all around this city, and you, you are crying over a pile of yellow feathers?" She wished she had her mother's toughness instead of being so weak. But this was how she was made. She couldn't help it that she felt the suffering of others—kin and strangers, creatures that speak and creatures that can't speak—inside herself, as though the membrane separating her body from the world was thin and porous.

Her grandmother said, "Shakar is in heaven now, *yavrum*. The canaries are singing with the angels. Just imagine their beautiful songs. And they can fly wherever they want. There are no cages in heaven. There is no fighting and no war. In heaven, the body is made perfect by God, and no one is ever sick or tired or sad."

But Vera was still sad. She would never hear Shakar's song again, and she would never see him peering at her with one bright eye. She would likely never see Alex again. Their departure was looming over her like a sharp-taloned hawk.

Their mother said, "You three listen to me. I don't want any trouble at your grandmother's. Armen, don't complain that we're traitors and scoundrels. Raffi, don't boast about the wonderful things you will have in America. And Vera, don't start spouting water like a spigot."

As they were walking over the bridge, it was so hot and humid that Vera felt as though she were inside the mouth of a giant dog. She smelled the stench of the Bourj Hammoud garbage mountain, which had grown to great heights and blocked access to the shore.

They made their way along crowded sidewalks of Nor Marash toward the Joudigians' building. When they were within sight, Cousin Lena waved at them from the balcony.

The whole family had gathered on the grandparents' balcony where two tables were pushed together to make room for everyone. The grandmother and aunts had cooked for several days, and favorite dishes were lined up and down the middle of the table.

"*Aman!*" Medz Mairig said, as she kissed each of them. "Look at how big you all are. Vera, you're taller than me. Armen, you are getting a moustache! And look at Raffi, my smallest one, who is now such a handsome young man."

"Let's eat," their grandfather said, taking his seat at the head of the table. "We have to get back to the shop soon, and the pilaf is getting cold."

Amo Nubar said, "In this weather? Nothing is getting cold. In fact, everything is melting, including me."

Currents of conversation circulated around the table along with the bowls and platters. Vera sat with Lena on one side and Raffi on the other. Vera observed the shade of Lena's red lipstick and the way her cousin had applied kohl eyeliner. Vera still wasn't allowed to wear makeup. She wasn't even allowed to shave her legs, although her mother had promised that when they got to New Jersey, she could do both.

"Diran, when are you and Araxi deserting us?" Amo Nubar asked.

"Deserting?" Mairig said sharply.

Baba answered, "We're going by taxi to Jounieh on Sunday, taking a boat from there to Cyprus, and then we fly to New York."

Medz Mairig said, "On Sunday, people drive to the ports with their suitcases, or, when it's open, they go to the airport. Sunday is the saddest day of the week. What will become of our people?"

Their mother said, "So I'm responsible for the fate of the Armenian people?"

"No one is blaming you," said Medz Mairig.

"Everyone is blaming me," Mairig said, her voice rising. "I can't stand it anymore. If something happened to one of my children, you might as well tear my heart from my chest. It's complete insanity to stay in this madhouse."

Her mother's words hung in the air like a bluish cloud of cigarette smoke over the silent table.

Vera, who had her sketchpad open on her lap, was drawing the nests of electrical wires that hung draped from house to house on their street. She, Taline, and Seta were sitting on chairs outside the stationery store.

"I can't believe this is your last day," Seta said to Vera.

"You're going to miss having Baron Vartan for English. He's supposed to be the best teacher in the school," Taline said.

Seta said, "You mean the handsomest."

Taline sighed. "He looks just like Adiss, doesn't he? With that smile and those black, black eyes."

"You want to see my drawings?" Vera asked.

The girls leaned in, and Vera turned the leaves of her sketchpad. She had drawn each room of her house, its exterior, the rooftop garden, and the view of Bourj Hammoud from the roof. Then came the streets of Nor Hadjin, the church, both inside and out, the avenue, and the steps leading up to Getawi. Next were the portraits.

"You can choose one to keep," Vera said.

"I want that one," said Taline. It was drawn from a photograph of the three girls at Vera's sixth birthday party. They wore conical paper hats and their Sunday dresses. Smiling broadly, they were all missing their top front teeth.

Vera carefully detached the page, handing it to Taline.

Next was a caricature she had made of the Badveli at the pulpit in the school's chapel. His enormous bald head was crowned with a tiny halo, his eyebrows were two black caterpillars, his nose was a honking beak, and little wings sprouted from his shoulders.

Seta laughed. "He would love that. Should I take that one?"

Vera said, "I think you'll prefer the next one."

It was a drawing made from another photo of the three of them, this time sitting on the bench outside the candy shop. They were about ten years old. They didn't know that the war was about to begin. Seta's hair was in two plaits on either side of her thin face, Taline had a white kerchief tied over her curls, and Vera was sitting between them. They were holding up large caramel lollipops.

That evening Vera eyed the food that her grandmother had arrayed on the kitchen table before them. She had cooked their favorite dishes. Vera felt queasy, but she forced herself to eat. Her chewing was mechanical and joyless.

Their mother said, "As soon as we find our own house, your father will build a wooden fort for Raffi."

"It's going to be a playhouse," Raffi said. "With a swing."

Armen said, "You already told us this a hundred times."

Their father said, "Look at the beautiful meal your grandmother made."

"The last supper," Vera said.

Mairig said, "Stop being an ungrateful wretch."

Vera burst into tears.

Their mother jumped up from the table. "I'm going out."

After the dishes were washed, Vera climbed to the roof with her grandmother. With rainwater collected in tin pails, they watered the herbs, flowers, and flowering vines. She would miss the fragrance of the jasmine and the oleander, and the bright trumpets of the potted hibiscus tree her grandmother looked after as carefully as you might tend a baby. They watered the tomatoes, peppers, and eggplants that were growing in clay pots.

In the distance, Vera could see the bridge spanning the river and the shelf of clouds towering over Bourj Hammoud where the Joudigians were sitting on their balconies on this summer evening. Soon the sun would go down. Soon it would be night. Her final night in Beirut.

When it was time for bed Vera pulled on a frayed nightdress. Her grandmother sat on the edge of her own bed and released her long hair from its bun. Vera sat behind her, taking the silver-plated brush with yellowed bristles. She brushed her grandmother's thinning gray hair.

"Thank you, *yavrum*," Medz Mama said.

"Who will do this for you?" Vera asked.

"Oh, you know this is nice, but I can brush my own hair," she said.

Medz Mama turned off the flashlight and they lay side by side in the dark room they had shared since Vera could remember.

Vera rolled from one side to the other. She listened to the ticking of the clock on the nightstand, a steady beat that often helped her to fall asleep. But now the sound was as ominous as the timer on a car bomb.

Vera must have sighed because the grandmother sat up and turned on the flashlight. "I also can't sleep."

"I don't want to go," Vera said.

The grandmother stood up and went to the dresser. She pulled a small black box from the top drawer. She sat down on Vera's bed.

"I was going to give this to you tomorrow. Here, open it," she said.

Vera hinged open the top of the velvet box and found a pair

of gold drop earrings with small red stones in the shape of a flower.

"Your grandfather gave those to me when your father was born," the grandmother said. "The stones are garnet. I haven't worn them in years."

"Thank you," Vera said. "They are very beautiful."

Vera closed the box and set it on the nightstand between the beds. Soon her chest was heaving, and tears were streaming down her face. Her grandmother rubbed her back, making small circles between her shoulder blades.

"*Yavrum*," her grandmother said. "I have two more things to give you." She went again to the dresser and came back to the bed holding a folded white handkerchief that was edged with blue lace. She carefully opened the cloth and lifted a black feather and handed it to Vera.

Vera held the white shaft in one hand and ran her finger along the feather's black edge.

Her grandmother said, "The second gift is this feather, and the third is a story that goes with it." She enfolded the plume in the hankie and placed it on the nightstand.

When they were again in their beds, Medz Mama switched off the light and said into the dark, "You grandfather and I each wandered out of the desert, leaving our dead behind us. We were alone, but eventually we found each other. Together, we made a new life and a new family in Nor Hadjin. Your grandfather sawed and hammered the beams for this house. And with the help of our neighbors, he put up the walls and the roof. He made the kitchen table where we eat, and he made the chairs. I sewed the cushions for the chairs and the curtains for the windows. I planted my garden in containers on the roof. This is where your father and his brothers were born and learned to walk. This is where you and your brothers arrived like gifts. When we buried your grandfather, part of me was buried with him, and part of him is still here in this home."

Vera asked, "His ghost?"

"A ghost. A spirit. A memory. His hands touched each plank in this house."

"But we need you," Vera said.

"Exile is a burning shirt I will never wear again."

The night was hot, and Vera kicked the sheet to the bottom of the bed.

Her grandmother said, "And now the rest of the story. I have told you many tales about Sosi's life in Hadjin, but never how the story ends."

Her grandmother's steady voice filled the small room. Vera saw the mountains encircling Hadjin, and the town nestled in the valley. She saw its houses built into the side of the hills. She saw the cobbled streets, the water fountains, and the orchards. She heard church bells ringing. She smelled bread baking in the communal oven, and she felt the sun on her face in the garden. And then her grandmother told Vera for the first time about what had happened to Sosi and her family when they were forced to leave Hadjin with little more than the clothes on their backs.

When the tale was finished, Vera was weeping, and her grandmother reached across the gap between the beds for her hand.

"Sosi was your sister," Vera said.

"Yes," Medz Mama answered.

"Why didn't you tell me before?" she asked.

"It was too heavy a burden for a child. But you are old enough now and can make of it what you will. I'm weary, my girl. We must sleep."

Vera lay on her back, and she saw above her on the dark ceiling rows of small children, their large eyes melancholy, their hair shorn for lice, and the clothes hanging loosely on their scrawny bodies. Her grandmother was one of those children. Her other grandparents as well. And there had been thousands upon thousands of them, without homes, without parents, some too young to remember their own names. And these were the lucky ones, the ones who had survived. Land of Armenians, land of orphans.

She knew by the slow, steady breathing that her grandmother had fallen asleep. Vera must think of something else or else she would be awake all night.

It was a Sunday afternoon, and her family was riding the streetcar all the way to Raouché. Raffi had just learned to walk, and their father carried him on his shoulders. Their grandmother held Vera's hand, while Armen raced ahead of them along the Corniche. Baba bought them ice cream cones; Vera's was chocolate and Armen's was pistachio. They sat on a bench with a view of Pigeon Rocks. The ocean was wide and blue with small whitecaps dancing on the tops of the waves. The waves rolled against the rocky shore, one after the next and the next.

It was almost sunset when they reached the Casino du Liban. With suitcases in hand, they filed toward the dock where a fishing boat was moored. Vera watched the sun slide toward the water on the orange and pink streaked horizon. There were several other families waiting on the wooden dock. When their turn came, their father handed across the bags, and one by one they climbed aboard.

The motor chugged as black plumes of diesel smoke wafted above. The sky darkened, and the boat nosed toward the open sea. Their father stood at the stern facing the receding shore where lights climbed up the hills toward the stars, which were arrayed like a net across the sky.

One of the men on the boat had a transistor radio turned on full volume. Fairuz was singing "I Love You Lebanon." The singer's words of love and loss slid into Vera's ear and down her throat until they grasped her heart like two hands.

Vera left the bench where her mother and brothers were seated and went to stand beside her father.

"What a voice that woman has. What a soul. When Fairuz sings, the whole world weeps," he said. He brushed the back of his hand across his eyes.

They turned their backs to the distant shore, and Vera saw the lights of a cruise ship glittering like a tiered necklace in the dark ahead of them. Their boat continued toward the anchored ship, and when it stilled its motor as they pulled alongside, the boat rocked, the waves slapping against its sides. The bags were heaved up, and one by one they climbed aboard.

The fishing boat captain and his mate waved to them as they started their motor and turned back toward Lebanon, the wake churning behind them.

They were shepherded along the deck, and as they passed a row of brightly lit windows, Vera glimpsed a wood-paneled cabin where people in evening wear stood around a roulette wheel and blackjack tables. They were drinking cocktails, and Vera imagined she could hear the ice cubes shifting in their glasses, the spinning of the wheel as the ball clicked from slot to slot, and their laughter as they threw back their heads showing sharp white teeth.

The Serinossians filed down the stairs to a large cabin below deck that was lined with benches. Other families were already seated amidst their belongings. They found a spot for themselves on a slatted wooden bench, sliding their bags underneath.

It was too early yet to sleep, and the parents decided to go up to the deck for a little air.

"Watch your brothers," Mairig said to Vera.

"I bet he's going to smoke a cigarette," Raffi said.

Vera said, "He was crying on the boat."

"You saw him?" Armen asked.

"He said it was because of Fairuz," Vera said.

Raffi said, "He misses Medz Mama already."

Raffi reached under the bench, pulled out his suitcase and unlatched the top. "Look what she gave me." He held up a small glass jar filled with soil. "Nor Hadjin dirt." He unscrewed the lid. "Do you want to smell it?"

"Maybe later," Vera said.

Raffi then showed them a miniature wooden house. "Baba made this for her when he was twelve."

It was a small replica of their house, only five inches tall, but perfectly proportioned and intricately carved—the same double door, with grillwork over the street-level windows, wooden shutters over the second-floor windows, and an open terrace on the roof.

"What did she give you?" Raffi asked.

"A pair of earrings," Vera said. "And just before we left, she put the alarm clock from our bedroom in my suitcase." She didn't mention the feather that was in her skirt pocket.

Armen said, "Medz Babig's watch." He held up the octagonal gold timepiece. "It still works."

When their parents returned, their mother rolled a sweater for Raffi to put under his head as a pillow.

"Go to sleep," their mother said. "We won't arrive at the port until morning."

Then she settled on the bench, pulling a shawl over herself. Raffi was beside her with his head on her shoulder. Minutes later they were asleep, their mouths slack and slightly open. The father's snore was low and rhythmic.

Vera and Armen sat a little apart from the rest. Armen pressed his cheek to the window and gazed into the dark.

"What are you thinking?" she asked.

"Kevo and I talked about running away together," he said.

"Where would you have gone?"

He said, "Maybe Anjar. Maybe Aleppo."

"All the way to Syria?"

"We needed to go where they wouldn't think to look for us."

Vera said, "She would have searched until she found you, even if you were hiding in the last cave in the desert."

The ship's engine hummed as they moved farther and farther away from home.

When Vera woke up, her parents and her brothers were still

sleeping. She decided to climb to the deck. Leaning against the railing, she watched the sun emerge from the water. A solitary gull landed on the railing a few yards from where she stood. It had a brown head, a red beak and red legs, and black wing tips. It looked at her with one white-ringed eye, and then lifted off, winging toward the sun.

She moved to the bow. The sea glittered like a blue sapphire, and the sky was a slightly paler blue. There was a strip of land barely visible in the distance. Pulling the handkerchief from her skirt pocket, she unfolded the cloth. She held the shaft of the feather between her thumb and finger, raising it over the railing.

As she released the feather, she heard her grandmother's voice, "Give me wings that I might fly."

HADJIN

Gar ou chigar, gar ou chigar . . . There was and there was not a girl named Sosi who lived in a house at the edge of Hadjin, not far from the town's orchards and vineyards. Hadjin was an Armenian town nestled in a valley encircled on all sides by tall mountains, which provided shelter from the brigands and marauders who spread fear through the Taurus range. Two rivers and a large stream supplied the town's water, which ran cold from stone fountains in each quarter. Radiating from its center up into the hills, Hadjin's stone houses were built one upon the next into the rising slopes, resembling from afar a colony of nests made by alpine swifts.

Sosi lived in one of these stone houses near the edge of town with her parents, her grandparents, two younger twin brothers, and a small sister. The girl's parents had named her Sosi after the plane trees that were worshipped by Armenians since ancient times. The whispers of the trees' sacred leaves had often been used for divination. From a young age, Sosi spent long hours in the garden near her family's home. In the fair months, she helped weed, water, and harvest the vegetables. She fed the chickens, collecting from them the speckled brown eggs that her mother used in her baking.

Her mother was known for her fine breads and pastries. For Easter, she made Hadjin's traditional *digin* sweet bread using butter, white flour, yeast, and sour cherry seeds she ground with a brass mortar and pestle. Once the dough had risen twice, had been cut and then shaped, she brushed a beaten egg across the top of the loaves before sprinkling them with sesame seeds. Sosi went with her mother to the nearby baker where their tray was put into the communal oven. The scent of baking bread drifted through the neighborhood, an announcement of the coming feast. Sosi gathered more eggs, and her grandmother boiled some of them with onionskins to make them red and others with a special plant she harvested on the mountainside that turned them blue.

Sosi loved all manner of living things, from the wildflowers at the edge of the forest to the golden eagle that circled high overhead. After her schoolwork and chores were finished, Sosi sat on a large flat stone in one corner of the garden waiting for the small animals to emerge—the rabbit, the red squirrel, and the mouse. Day after day she sat on the stone until the animals grew used to her presence, and after a while even the birds would approach. She saved crusts of bread for them, and eventually some of the sparrows landed on her wrist to take crumbs from her extended palm.

In the garden, in the vineyard, in the forest, and on the cliff faces of the mountains, she observed the birds carefully, learning from her grandfather their names and studying their ways. Soon she could tell one from another—the magpie from the raven, the rock pigeon from the turtle dove, the stork from the crane. After a time, she began to recognize certain birds as individuals with features that distinguished them from others of their kind, in the way that each member of her family had a distinct character. Her favorite among them was the gray wallcreeper that clung to the rocks and cliffs. It was in almost constant motion, hopping sideways and probing with its sharp beak for insects hiding in cracks in the rock. When it flicked its crimson wings with white spots open, Sosi was reminded of a butterfly.

In the springtime, Hadjin's meadows, pastures, and mountain slopes were bright with flowers. In the orchard near their home, the pomegranate, cherry, mulberry, and apple trees blossomed each in their time. Sosi's grandmother knew the names of the flowers and plants, as well as their healing properties. When she took Sosi with her to collect ingredients for herbal remedies, the girl made garlands and bouquets to bring back to the house. As the spring progressed, different wildflowers appeared, starting with the blue and white glory-of-the-snow, followed by the purple crocus, the carpet of scarlet poppies, the star-like blossoms of the asphodel, bright yellow buttercups, tiny forget-me-nots, and many more.

Sosi understood that each living thing had a name, and she wanted to learn what to call each flower, grass, and insect. Her mother knew many of the names, and her grandmother knew even more, but neither of them knew them all. In response to Sosi's incessant questions, her grandmother said, "The Creator made them, and only the Creator knows the name of each and every one."

Sosi's grandfather had told her that there were many other languages than the two her family used, and she marveled at the splendid and difficult work of choosing names for each living thing in all the languages that were spoken in the world.

Sosi's grandmother added, "The Creator knows your name, the number of hairs that there are on your head, and the exact measure of days that you will walk upon this earth."

In the evening, her grandfather told Sosi and her younger siblings stories about the other animals that lived in the forest: the roe deer, the wild goat, red fox, lynx, gray wolf, and the brown bear. He had tracked all of them in his younger days as a hunter, but Sosi did not want to hear about the hunt. She wanted only to learn how these creatures lived in the forest, scrambling up and down the mountain slopes in and

around Hadjin. Most of all she loved listening to her grandfather's tales of long-ago times when animals had conversed
with humans.

In her grandfather's stories, a flying horse might give advice
to a young man in his quest for a bride, or a fox might trick
a stupid man into bartering away his cow. A little boy might
be transformed into a lamb, or a nightingale's feather would
miraculously restore the sight of a blind girl.

In Hadjin, birds were believed to have magical properties.
One day, Sosi accompanied her grandmother to the market,
where the old woman bought a white dove from a man sell-
ing birds. Sosi noticed that the snow-white bird had a single
black tail feather that distinguished it from the other doves.
They carried the dove home in a wicker cage, and early the
next morning, the grandmother and the girl brought the cage
to the edge of the forest. Her grandmother opened the cage
door, reaching in carefully for the dove and placing it in Sosi's
hands. Sosi felt its small heart beating against her palms. It
turned its head to the side, looking up at her with one dark
eye ringed with gold.

Her grandmother said, "Hold the dove in your right hand,
and circle it around your head three times."

Sosi followed her grandmother's instructions.

Her grandmother went on, "Now, my girl, say, 'Be free and
carry our troubles away,' open your hand, and let it fly."

Sosi repeated the words, loosened her grip on the dove, and
tossed it skyward. She watched it as it flew higher and disappeared over the tops of the trees.

"Where will it go?" she asked her grandmother.

"It has gone to build a nest," her grandmother said. "May
God watch over our dove, and may He watch over us as well."

Some weeks later, when Sosi went to the orchard to pick

mulberries, she noticed a white dove sitting in a branch of the tree. From the single black feather in its tail, she recognized it was the same one that she and her grandmother had bought at the market and released.

"Greetings, Sosi," it said.

This was the first time that Sosi had herself heard an animal speak, but she was not surprised. She answered, "Greetings to you, white dove."

"I have sought you out," it said, "because a time of troubles is coming. Out of gratitude for your having given me my freedom, I want to present you with a gift that will help you in your hour of need."

"What kind of trouble, friend?" Sosi asked.

"It is not for me to tell you what lies ahead, but I am here to give you this feather, and to instruct you in how to use it."

Here the black tail feather dropped on the ground in front of Sosi. She leaned over to pick it up. It was smooth and sleek, and to all appearances an ordinary feather.

"You must wrap the feather in a bit of cloth," the dove said.

Sosi pulled a handkerchief from her pocket—it was a square of white cotton that her grandmother had edged with white lace. Sosi's initial was embroidered in blue on one corner.

"Will this do?" she asked.

"That is perfect," it said.

Sosi placed the black feather in the middle of the white cloth, carefully folding in the corners until the feather was hidden.

"Put it in your pocket and always carry it with you. When you sleep, put it under your pillow."

"Is there anything more?"

"When the time of woe comes upon your people, there will be a moment when your own suffering will be great. In that moment, you must hold the feather by its quill, close your eyes and say, 'Give me wings that I might fly.'"

"And is this magic for me alone?" Sosi asked. "What about my family? What about the other people in my town?"

"I am not powerful enough to save more than you. But I promise that your grandmother, who purchased my freedom, will make her way to heaven before the time of strife."

Sosi told no one about her meeting with the dove, but she did exactly as it had instructed. And when sometime later her grandmother fell ill and took to her bed, Sosi thought that the hard times the dove had predicted were soon to be upon them.

Before dawn on Sunday, the beadle walked through town carrying a staff in one hand and a candle in the other. He rapped three times on the door of each house with his wooden staff, singing his summons to the mass.

> Oh, you good Christians
> Come to the church service
> Do not sleep or slumber
> Open your ears, do not remain deaf
> Do not tarry, it is time for holy prayers
> Oh, you good Christians
> Come to church

Later in the morning the church bells pealed, calling worshippers to the service. The church interior was lit by candles in sconces on the wall and oil lamps that hung on long chains from the ceiling. The priest in his embroidered vestments and the altar boy swinging a gold censer paced up and down the nave. Incense floated above their heads, rising like prayers to heaven.

Sosi sat in the pew with her parents, her grandfather, and her younger siblings through the long service. Her grandmother, who was still unwell, had stayed home that morning. When her little sister grew restless, Sosi led her by the hand to the back of the sanctuary where they looked at the candles burning in the metal stand. Sosi dropped a coin in the box, took a candle, and, thinking of her grandmother at home sick in bed, lit it from the flame of another one, planting it in the sand alongside the other candles.

The grandmother did not get well, and when the crocuses were blooming, they buried her in the family plot in the church cemetery. A few weeks later, Sosi's father was arrested along with many of the men of Hadjin. He did not return, and his disappearance added to the family's sorrow. When the deportation orders were issued soon thereafter, Sosi understood that the dove's prophecy was being fulfilled.

Sosi helped her mother and grandfather pack what belongings they could carry. As the eldest of the four children, Sosi felt responsible for the care of her younger sister because her mother and her grandfather were distracted by the grief of their recent losses. Her twin brothers were sturdy and relied on each other, but her little sister was bewildered and afraid.

The Armenians were driven out of Hadjin like sheep, forced to travel by foot on the Kiraz mountain road. The first night, Sosi, her family, and the other deportees of Hadjin lay down by the side of the road to sleep, the sky above them a black cloth through which tiny pricks of light could be seen. Sosi unfolded the handkerchief that she carried in her pocket and smoothed the black feather. She wondered how she would know when it was time to call upon its magic. She wondered also whether she would be capable of using the feather to save herself alone. Who would take care of her little sister?

The journey was difficult, so difficult in fact that each day the column of Armenians grew smaller as people died during the night or fell by the wayside. Food and water grew scarce. They lost Sosi's grandfather. And the twins were taken by a passing Kurdish Agha who pulled them onto the mule tied to his horse and promised to feed them and treat them as his own.

One morning while they were still in the mountains, Sosi woke up before her mother and sister and walked toward a cliff face that rose on one side of the road. There she saw a wallcreeper hopping and fluttering across the rock. Sosi was surprised that despite the misery of their lot, in her burning heart she could still be awed by the beauty of this creature.

Then the wallcreeper perched on a rock and spoke to her.

"My friend the white dove has a message for you," it said.

"What message, dear friend?" Sosi asked.

"The white dove wants you to know that when you use the feather's power to save yourself, your small sister will not be left alone. All the birds she passes on her journey will watch over her, help her, feed her, and she will find her way. In fact, she will live a long life, she will be a mother and a grandmother to many children."

"And my own mother?" Sosi asked.

"Dear girl, your mother died during the night. That is why the white dove sent me."

And with that the wallcreeper took flight, rising over the cliff face and disappearing.

Sosi returned to where she had left her mother and sister, finding that what the wallcreeper had said about her mother was true. There was nothing to do but pretend that their mother was asleep. Sosi clasped her sister's small hand, and they continued their long march with the other Armenians of Hadjin, who were now family to each other.

The remnant band eventually arrived at their destination: a barren place in the Syrian Desert. The heat was considerable, the food was scarcer still, and water was hard to come by. Each day Sosi devoted herself to find something to eat and to drink for her sister and herself. Some days she was successful. Some days they went without so much as a crust of bread, and they sucked on pebbles.

One afternoon when the shadows were growing long, marauding Turkish soldiers moved through the desert encampment, kidnapping girls. Sosi, thin as she was and barely thirteen years old, caught the eye of one such soldier. As he approached Sosi and her sister, they started to run, but he chased behind them, grabbing Sosi by the wrist. Her little sister wailed and screamed, gripping the frayed hem of Sosi's skirt as the soldier pulled her away. The little sister fell to the ground sobbing as Sosi was dragged farther and farther away.

Sosi struggled with the soldier, and when she realized she was unable to wrest herself from his grasp, she knew the time had come. She reached her free hand into her dress pocket, opened the ragged handkerchief, and held the black feather between her thumb and forefinger. She took one last glance at her sister, closed her eyes, and whispered, "Give me wings that I might fly."

The little sister was still weeping and watching in terror, when suddenly Sosi disappeared. In her place, a white dove rose above the soldier's head. Bewildered, he looked wildly around for the girl who had been in his hands only seconds before.

The dove flew toward the little sister, and the little girl heard it say, "Don't be afraid, Silva. Now I must fly with my kin, but know that all the birds of the desert, the field, and the forest will protect and watch over you. They have promised me that you will live to be an old woman with many grandchildren."

With that, the white dove rose higher and higher, flying toward the sun that was pinned like a burning flower to the sky.

That night, Silva slept next to another mother from Hadjin and her surviving son. "You are my daughter now, little one," the mother said. And while Silva slept, she dreamed of the beautiful white dove that her sister had become. The dove soared into the mountains high above the Armenian town of Hadjin, which will always remain our beloved homeland.

Three apples fell from heaven, one for the storyteller, one for the listener, and one for the person who understands this tale.

Ժողովուրդիս համար

GLOSSARY

Agoump: Club

Amo: Uncle (borrowed from Arabic)

Anoushig: Sweetie

Baba, Babig: Dad, Daddy

Badveli: Reverend (Protestant)

Baron: Mister

Dashnak: Armenian Revolutionary Federation (political party)

Digin: Mrs.

Hunchak: Social Democratic Hunchakian Party (Armenian political party)

Joudig: Little chick

Kataeb: Phalangist Party (Lebanese Christian)

Mairig: Mama, Mommy

Medz Mairig, Medz Mama: Grandma

Medz Baba, Medz Babig, Medz Hairig: Grandpa

Shirkets: An informal women's lending society

Sirov: With love

Tantig: Auntie (borrowed from French)

ACKNOWLEDGMENTS

Profound gratitude to the friends who opened their hearts and their homes in Lebanon to me: Antranig and Alina Dakessian, Nayiri Baboudjian and Raffi Bouchakjian, Arda and Raffi Karakashian, and Nigol Bezjian. Special thanks are due to the late Bedig Tchiftelian for devoting many hours to showing me around Bourj Hammoud and Nor Hadjin, and to Rosy Kuftedjian, who gave me several private tours of the Armenian neighborhoods of Beirut. Bedig and Rosy deepened my understanding of the geography, both physical and human, of Armenian Beirut.

Thank you to the friends and acquaintances who shared their Beirut stories with me: Elizabeth Aghazarian-Kajajian and her family, Lara Aharonian, Bishop Nareg Alemezian, Anny Bakalian, Paola Bakalian, Vartoug Balekjian, Vahe Berberian, Papken Boyadjian, Ara Dabandjian, Patil Dedeyan, Sahag Dedeyan, Sona Demirdjian, Maral Deyirmenjian, Levon Der Bedrossian, Maggie Goschin-Mangassarian, Houry Guedelekian, Nishan Kazazian, Hovaness Khatchadourian, the late Harry Koundakjian, Lola Koundakjian, Krikor Kradjian, Dr. Garabed Sahag Mahredjian, Arpiné Mangassarian, Seta Mangerian, Shahe Mankerian, Vatché Mankerian, Aline Manoukian, Markar and Suzy Melkonian, Khatchig Mouradian, Joanne Randa Nucho, Hagop Papazian, Nairi Papazian Saade, Ara Sanjian, Robert Setrakian, Vahé Tachjian, Lena Takvorian, Anais Tcholakian, Vasken Terzian, Anita Toutikian, Hrag Vartanian, Heghnar Zeitlian Watenpaugh, and Annie Yepremian.

BIOGRAPHICAL NOTE

Nancy Kricorian, who was born and raised in the Armenian community of Watertown, Massachusetts, is the author of four novels about post-genocide Armenian diaspora experience, including *Zabelle*, which was translated into seven languages, was adapted as a play, and has been continuously in print since 1998. Her essays and poems have appeared in *The Los Angeles Review of Books Quarterly*, *Guernica*, *Parnassus*, *Minnesota Review*, *The Mississippi Review*, and other journals. She has taught at Barnard, Columbia, Yale, and New York University, as well as with Teacher & Writers Collaborative in the New York City Public Schools and for the Palestine Writing Workshop in Birzeit. She has been the recipient of a New York Foundation for the Arts Fellowship, a Gold Medal from the Writers Union of Armenia, and the Anahid Literary Award. She lives in New York City.